Walter Inglisfield

Queen Elizabeth and Earl Leicester; a drama in five acts

Walter Inglisfield

Queen Elizabeth and Earl Leicester; a drama in five acts

ISBN/EAN: 9783337305796

Printed in Europe, USA, Canada, Australia, Japan

Cover: Foto ©Andreas Hilbeck / pixelio.de

More available books at **www.hansebooks.com**

A Drama in Five Acts.

BY

WALTER INGLISFIELD.

LONDON :

ELLIOT STOCK, 62, PATERNOSTER ROW, E.C.

1894.

THIS PLAY

Is respectfully dedicated

TO

RICHARD J. MIDDLETON, Esq., F.I. Inst., Etc.

QUEEN ELIZABETH AND EARL LEICESTER.

Dramatis Personæ.

QUEEN ELIZABETH.

THE EARL OF LEICESTER.

BURLEIGH, *Prime Minister.*

CHARLES IX., *King of France.*

DUC D'ALENÇON.

LA MOTTE FÉNELON, *French Ambassador.*

BISHOP AYLMER.

SIR CHARLES HATTON, *Vice-Chamberlain.*

THE EARL OF SUSSEX, *Lord Chamberlain.*

SIR THOMAS SMITH, *Ambassador at the French Court.*

WALSINGHAM, *Ambassador at the French Court.*

LORD LINCOLN.

SIR JOHN MELVILLE.

SIR THOMAS MOLE.

WHITLEY, *Hatton's servant.*

MURDERER.

CATHERINE DE MEDICIS.

COUNTESS OF ESSEX.

COUNTESS OF SHREWSBURY.

KATE ASHLEY.

LADY SHEFFIELD.

FRANCES HOWARD.

LADY LENNOX.

LADY FREEZE.

Courtiers, Ministers, Gentlemen, Citizens, etc.

ACT I.

SCENE I.—*A street in London.*

Enter EARL OF SUSSEX *and* BURLEIGH.

SUSSEX.

Hast thou no power to bend her will?

BURLEIGH.

'Twere easier to bend an iron rod
Than her too stubborn will.   I know no trick
That could accomplish it.   The more one tries
The stubborner she is; and gentle counsel
She changes to entreaty on our knees
That we may keep our heads.

SUSSEX.

                She angers me!

BURLEIGH.

Nay, be not angry, Sussex.

SUSSEX.

Not angry!
My God, her stubborn will incites our anger.

BURLEIGH.

Hsh!
If anyone should hear thee say such words,
I would not give a snapping for thy life.

SUSSEX.

My life!
Dost call this life, ruled by a woman's whims,
And we've no power to ope our mouths and say,
'This shall be' or 'That shall not be'? 'Tis not
A manly life to hold a silent tongue,
And let a foolish woman have her way.
I'll be a man and utter what I think,
E'en if I lose my head.

BURLEIGH.

Thou art too rash.
I would advise thee put a curb upon
Thy tongue, and blunt thy anger, my good lord.
The keenest knife needs carefullest handling.

SUSSEX.

What use is any knife that's blunt? We'd be
In sorry plight, my friend, if we possessed
No grinding stones.

BURLEIGH.

Ah, well !
If thou dost know what's best for thee I'll hold
My tongue.   I'd give my life if I could force
The queen to marry.

SUSSEX.

She must.
If without issue she should die, then woe
To England and our blessed Church !   Damned
    Rome
Would conquer and enslave us all.

BURLEIGH.

Methinks that Leicester is the cause of all
This obstinacy.

SUSSEX.

Oh, damn the hypocrite !
He's England's curse and scourge.

BURLEIGH.

Alas !

[*Exeunt* SUSSEX *and* BURLEIGH.

Enter TWO GENTLEMEN, *in conversation.*

1ST GENT.

If she should die, and leave no heir, the crown
Would then revert to Mary, Queen of Scots,
A Roman Catholic, and we should see

The bloody days of Mary's reign once more.
O think, my friend, what storm would burst upon
Our country, should our gracious majesty
Refuse to marry!

2ND GENT.

I see it all,
And sorrow heavily.   'Twere better she
Should marry Leicester than not wed at all.

1ST GENT.

God forbid!
I'd rather be enslaved to Rome than be
A subject to so vile and mean a king.
I marvel much her majesty can love
A wretch so worthless.

2ND GENT.

She loves his handsome face
And graceful form.

1ST GENT.

Which proves she is a woman, friend, of which
So many are in grievous doubt.   I would
To God she were less true a woman, we
Might live in more security than on
Deceitful whims.

[*Exeunt.*

Scene II.—*Westminster: a private apartment in the Palace.*

Enter Queen Elizabeth *alone.*

They'd force me marry, would they?   They would
        yoke
My queenly dignities with wifely cares?
God's death! I'll cure them. A husband! 'Sblood!
I'll husband them, and wife them, too! I'm placed
Above all men, and were a fool to share
My power with any masculine thing they call
A man!   I'll let no husband play the king
O'er me.   I know their real designs, but will
Outwit them all.   (*A pause*)
                And yet I would I were
A wife.   With all its power and dignities,
With all its pomp, and show, and splendour, 'tis
But hollow mockery.   I feed on naught
But husks.   I envy frequently the wives
Of artisans.   Though they are poor and mean,
They have their husbands' and their children's
        love.
I am no mother to my subjects, so
They cannot love me with sweet children's love.
I would I knew a deeper love.   I am
No longer young, but getting old and staid,
So cannot hope to find a husband who

Would love me for myself.   I'd give my crown
For such a love.

Enter LEICESTER.

What! thou rude man! wouldst dare to enter
    here?
Go from my presence, or thy head shall pay
The penalty of thy rash act.

LEICESTER (*kneeling*).

Pray pardon, most beloved majesty,
And be not angry with me, for 'twas love
That brought my footsteps close to thee.   I know,
Indeed, thou'rt in no happy mood, and that
Hath grieved me more than words can say.   I
    would
That thou wouldst let me share thy grief.   I long
To soothe it with the love I have for thee.
Pray, think, beloved majesty, what pain
It gives to me, what poignant misery,
To know thou art not happy.   There's no joy
For me when there is none for thee.   I know
What risk I run by thus intruding here ;
But love hath blinded me, and given me strength
To place my life in jeopardy.

ELIZABETH.

Ah, Leicester, thou'rt a skilful man, and know'st
Too well where my great weakness lies. 'Tis thou

Alone who canst with safety run the risk
Of my displeasure, but e'en thou canst go
Too far.   I warn thee, let this be thy last
Attempt.   Another time I shall not be
So quickly soothed.   Pray go, and flatter thee
That I have pardoned thy offence, and with
Content that I am far from suffering
What hath aroused thy fears.

LEICESTER.

Most gracious majesty, I give thee thanks.
I'm most unworthy thy great gentleness,
And thy too ready pardoning.   It will
But strengthen my great love for thee, and stir
My zeal to serve thee faithfully.

[*Exit* LEICESTER.

ELIZABETH.

Methinks there's one who hath true love for me.
And I love him.   Yea, I would marry him
If I could face the storm that then would burst
And rage all o'er the land.   Ofttimes I feel
My love would give me strength ; and then I
    doubt,
And fear o'ermasters me.   My crown is set
With many thorns, nor doth its splendour numb
The pain of wearing it.   I'm absolute ?
I have, indeed, the power o'er life and death.

But not the power to gain that happiness
Which those who fear me may enjoy. I am
More pitiable than they. I have no power
To crush their greatest joys, yet they have means
To make me lead a joyless life, and this
They use relentlessly. They'd urge me wed
A man I do not love! They shall not. Nay,
They shall not. They shall know that though I
    be
A woman and a queen, I have a will
That shall defeat their plans.

                      [Exit ELIZABETH.

SCENE III.—*The same. A room of state in the Palace. Lords spiritual and temporal, ministers, courtiers, etc., await in groups for the Queen. The throne at one end.* LORD SUSSEX *and* SIR CHARLES HATTON *are heard conversing.*

                SUSSEX.
Well, Hatton, why this grieving look?

                HATTON.
I see dark clouds ahead. I fear they'll burst
And injure us.

                SUSSEX.
                    I see them, too.
There's much to spoil in this assembly here.

HATTON.

Some fragile, dainty bodies, who can stand
But little stress of storm.

SUSSEX.

Mark Burleigh there.
He hath a drooping look.

HATTON.

Poor man !
He hath most weighty cares to bend his eyes.

SUSSEX.

Dost think she'll wed Anjou ?

HATTON.

I cannot tell.
No man has skill to read her changing mind.

SUSSEX.

He is a worthy match for her, methinks.
He's handsome, young, well-knit in form, and
bold.

HATTON.

In England many are more worthy her.

(*There is now a stir amongst the assembly as the Queen
is seen to enter with her attendants. She seats
herself on the throne.*)

ELIZABETH.

What is the meaning of this audience?
Lord Bishop, I do bid thee speak, for thou
Shouldst have a tend'rer conscience. I behold
Sheep's clothing here amongst the rest.

AYLMER.

Beloved and most gracious sovereign,
We, thy most humble subjects, deign to pray,
By aid of God's most holy grace, that thou
Wouldst in thy queenly wisdom—for, indeed,
Thou art most wise above all queens that e'er
Have reigned—think it now time to wed.

ELIZABETH.

                        Ha!

AYLMER.

Think not, most gracious majesty, that we
Presume, and would dictate to thee. I swear
By God's most Holy Writ we do it out
Of love for thee and for the Church of which
Thou art the worthy head. Thy enemies
Rejoice in thy virginity. If thou
Wouldst marry, it would crush their fondest hopes,
And take their strength away. Think, mighty
    queen,
Of that great empire thou dost rule, whose name
Is known, whose power is felt, the wide world o'er.

To thee it owes its mightiness ; 'tis thou
Who keep'st intact the sandy atoms which
Compose it, and which could with ease be rent
Asunder by thy death.

ELIZABETH.

'Sblood !
Speak not to me of death.   If thou wouldst have
Me listen to thy speech, I counsel thee
To preach no funeral harangue.

AYLMER.

I crave thy pardon, gracious majesty.

ELIZABETH.

I pardon thee
With right good will.   Thou art an honest man,
But art the dupe of others who have used
Thy mouth to speak their thoughts.   I know their
    minds.
They would coerce me into marriage.   Ha !
They think 'twould be more manly to obey
A king.   They like no woman rule.   They would
Forget abroad who governs them at home.
They like it not to take commands from one
Whom they regard inferior to themselves.

SUSSEX (*aside to* HATTON).

She fishes well.

HATTON (*aside to* SUSSEX).

The holy priest doth recognise the bait.
He's tasted it aforetime.

AYLMER.

                    Nay, mighty queen,
We do rejoice, and thank our God that He
Hath sent from heaven a queen so wise and
    gentle,
So fair and beautiful, whose piety
Hath been a good example to us all.
No king could be so fit to govern us.
'Tis we who show no worthiness to be
The subjects of so great a queen.   If thrones
Are only made secure if built upon
A nation's love and gratitude, then thine
Need never fear the fiercest storm.   We have
For thee the veneration which is due
To those most wise.   Then, think not, gracious
    madam,
We scorn thee or thy government, and wish
To have a king.   Nay ! nay !   God knows it is
Not so.   Thou doest us a grievous wrong.
We'd have thee wed, indeed, for thine own sake,
And for thy truer happiness.

ELIZABETH.

I thank thee, my good lord. Thou speakest well.
Thou hast a tongue most eloquent. But I
Would bid thee cease, not tire thyself, and store
Thy eloquence for thy professional work.

> [*Exeunt Queen and attendants.*

SCENE IV.—*Outside the Palace.*

Enter LEICESTER *and* BURLEIGH.

LEICESTER.

I tell thee she will marry none but me.
I know her mind on this too well to fear
She'll wed a foreigner. I swear by Heaven
She shall not marry any Duc d'Anjou.
I tell thee, Burleigh, I shall yet be king,
And woe to my sworn enemies ! Methinks
They'll tremble then and feel their heads quite
    loose.

BURLEIGH.

Thou know'st I am no enemy of thine.

LEICESTER.

            Thou art too sly, my lord,
And hast too great a fondness for thy head,

And for the power thou wield'st. But some are
    rash,
And show their hasty tempers and their spleen ;
But I will trip them up, by God !

                         [*Exeunt both.*

Enter SUSSEX *and* HATTON.

SUSSEX.

I say she must be saved. She doth refuse
To save herself, so we must do it.

HATTON.

What ! save her when the wolf is at her throat ?

SUSSEX.

Yea, even then.

HATTON.

But she will cling to it. She likes its bite.
To-day a man of courage dared to say
She sought her death, yet she insulted him.
How shall we save her, then ?

SUSSEX.

                  I see a way.
She was not in a happy mood to-day.
The bishop's weighty words will not be lost,
I'll warrant thee. She'll deeply ponder them.

HATTON.

> Pray God she will
And find them curing medicine.

Re-enter LEICESTER *alone.*

SUSSEX.

Here comes the traitor.   (*To* LEICESTER) Thou
    art the cause,
Detested hypocrite, why she hath scorned
Our bishop's holy words.   Thou art the cause
Of her displeasure—thou, whose damned conceit
Would have her for thyself.

LEICESTER.

> Be calm, my lord.
This haughty anger is most ill-advised.
I thought thou wert a wiser man.   Thou hast
Not wisdom e'en to save thy head.

SUSSEX.

Nor hadst thy father, upstart, and the wisdom
Which he did lack, which lopped his head, his
    son
Hath well inherited.   Thy father was
A fool, but thou'rt a heartless knave.

LEICESTER.

But yet a knave too much for Sussex.   Ha!

2

SUSSEX.

Wilt thou dare imitate our gracious queen !
Thou art not fit to tie her blessed shoes.

LEICESTER.

But fit to be her husband, so she thinks.

SUSSEX.

Thou villain ! cur !

LEICESTER.

     My lord will rue these hasty words.
I bear thee no ill-will.   My happiness
Hath eased my temper, sir.

SUSSEX.

I'd like to crack thy swollen head.

                [*Exit* LEICESTER.

HATTON.

          He speaks the truth.
Thou art too hasty, my good lord.   We cannot
Defeat the devil by high words.   Our wrath
Is oft the fire with which he tortures us.

SUSSEX.

     Oh, damn the cur !
Shall such a villain wed our noble queen ?
I'll kill him first.   Yea, with my life I'll try
To save my country and my queen.

              [*Exeunt both.*

SCENE V. — *Room in the house of the* COUNTESS OF ESSEX. *The* COUNTESS *discovered alone.*

COUNTESS OF ESSEX.

My lord is late,
An hour beyond his time. Why should I feel
This strange disquietude ? I love him, yea,
With all my heart, but can I be his wife ?
The queen doth love him, too, and I am sure
Would marry Dudley if she dared. If she
But knew we have these secret interviews
Nor he nor I would be alive a day. It is,
I fear, the risk we run that makes me feel
This dread.

Enter LEICESTER *disguised.*

Ah, thou art come ! Thou'rt late.

(*He kisses her.*)

LEICESTER.

And didst thou fear I would not come ?

COUNTESS OF ESSEX.

Methought
Thou wast detained elsewhere.

LEICESTER.

Ha ! ha !
(*He caresses her.*)

Be not so jealous, love.   'Twas not the queen
Who made me late, but Sussex, that proud pup,
Did bark at me and danced about my heels.

COUNTESS OF ESSEX.

Methinks he'll trip thee up some day.

LEICESTER.

Not till I kick him first.

COUNTESS OF ESSEX.

What makes him hate thee so?

LEICESTER.

'Tis jealousy,
And from the cause that makes thee jealous.

COUNTESS OF ESSEX.

He thinks thou'lt be above him?

LEICESTER.

Methinks I am already.

COUNTESS OF ESSEX.

He could not bide thee king.

LEICESTER.

Nor couldst thou.
He thinks I'll wed the queen.   That is thy fear,
So why dost thou not hate me, too?

COUNTESS OF ESSEX.

Because thou lov'st me, but thou hast no love
For him. Yet sometimes I'm in grievous doubt
Thou lov'st her best.

LEICESTER.

    Come ! come !
Thou art more beautiful, and hast a heart
More soft, a disposition far more sweet.
Thou art a woman, she is more a man
Than many men. I ofttimes doubt her sex,
So masculine is she at times. 'Tis thou,
Alone, I love. The fairest in the land
Art thou. To think that I would choose the
  stone
Uncut, when I may have the polished gem !

COUNTESS OF ESSEX.

Thou couldst be tempted to exchange if it
Were given with a crown.

LEICESTER.

     Fear not.
She will not marry me. I said she has
The courage of a man, but even she
Would dread to face her subjects' scorn and
  wrath.
'Tis wise of me to humour her. I know

She's in my power, and I were a fool
To make her free and thus enslave myself.
So thou and I must rest content awhile
To love and wed in secrecy.

SCENE VI.—*Guest-room in the house of the* COUNTESS OF SHREWSBURY. *Guests assembled.*

COUNTESS OF SHREWSBURY.

Now, Lady Lennox, what hast thou to say?
Thou art a near relation of the queen,
And so should know her secret acts.

LADY LENNOX.

Alas! that I were not so near in blood!
She fears and hates her kin, and seeks excuse
To thrust them into prison, as she did me.

COUNTESS OF SHREWSBURY.

                    Come! come!
No sighing over that.   Thou'rt free, and not
In prison, wench, nor would she dare again
To put thee there.   So speak thy mind, and say
If this be true of her.

LADY LENNOX.

                    Alas!
How should I know?   I'm never near the court

To hear the gossip spoken there.   Besides,
She never would confess to such a deed
To anyone.

COUNTESS OF SHREWSBURY.

   I am convinced 'tis true.
She's done in public what doth not become
The lowest woman, let alone a queen,
So I am sure in secrecy, with such
A man, her modesty would not restrain
Her acts.

Enter SIR CHRISTOPHER HATTON.

Here comes the man who can confirm the story.

HATTON.

What is the latest riddle, pray?   Sweet ladies,
If I can solve it I'm at your commands.

COUNTESS OF SHREWSBURY.

Without parade, it is that Leicester was
Observed to come from out the queen's own
   room,
Where no one is allowed to go but she.

HATTON.

    Great God !
And is it come to this ?   That he was there
To no good purpose is to be inferred,

But would the queen give countenance to his
Deep vice, she who doth set herself to be
A type of chaste virginity ?   Nay, nay,
It cannot be.   It is not true.   How didst
Thou hear of this ?

COUNTESS OF SHREWSBURY.

Thou need'st must guess.
My ears would not have heard it had there been
No cause for it.   They are not blind at court,
Nor are they fools, although her majesty
May think them so.

HATTON.

But they are idle gossipers, and fond
Of tattle.   They've invented this to serve
Some purpose of their own.   Perchance they
    have
Some spite against the queen, or, likelier,
Against the villain Leicester, for who doth
Not hate this man ?   The queen is innocent.
'Twas he who forced himself into her presence,
For he is bold and bad enough.   No doubt,
Through love for him she's hushed it up.   She is,
I'll warrant thee, a chaste and virtuous queen.

COUNTESS OF SHREWSBURY.

Ah ! Sir Christopher,
If all had faith in her as thou, she'd have

A merry time of it. I am convinced,
From what I know of woman and the queen,
That she is not so virtuous as she
Would seem to be. My Lady Freeze doth share
My thoughts? (*Turns to her.*)

LADY FREEZE.

Yea, indeed
I could not swear the queen was virtuous.
I would not be so vile a hypocrite.
The woman who hath secret talks with such
A man as Leicester, though she be a queen,
Must needs give way to overpow'ring lust.
That is the nature of their love.

Enter BURLEIGH.

COUNTESS OF SHREWSBURY.

Ha! ha!
No longer shall we be in doubt. Here comes
A man who can enlighten us.

BURLEIGH.

Yea! yea!
I can enlighten ye. I have some news
Which will rejoice ye all.

COUNTESS OF SHREWSBURY.

Pray tell it us.

BURLEIGH.

The queen hath sent a letter to the duke
To say she will not marry him. So all
Is o'er. Our efforts are in vain, and we
Must cringe to Leicester's insolence.

HATTON.

                                      Not I.
I will defy him ; yea, by God, I will.

BURLEIGH.

We all, with safety, may defy him here ;
But in his presence, Chris ?

HATTON.

I will defy him to his face. I hate
The cur, and can no longer bear his yelps.

LADY FREEZE.

But what about her majesty, who loves
Him so ? Thou canst not injure him, if he
Should screen himself behind her back. Thou
    wouldst
Not sneer at him, but at the queen, and she
Would frown on thee, to thy sore grief.

HATTON.

                    I care not for the queen.
If she will seek the ruin of herself

And country, spite of sage advice, then she
Must needs incur the scorn of all.

LADY FREEZE.

Tut !
Thou know'st her frown hath often made thee ill.
Thou'rt ne'er so happy as when she doth smile
On thee.   Thy joyous face would make us think
'Twas pleasant summer time.

HATTON.

Thou hast a biting tongue, my Lady Freeze.
So sharp a weapon should be used with mercy.

LADY FREEZE.

Nay, nay.
It is the only weapon we possess,
And that is weak compared with man's great
     strength
Of body, which is used relentlessly
On us, to keep us in our place, as he
Is wont to say.   My counsel to my sex
Is this : Until your husband shows ye by
Example how ye should be merciful,
Treat him with harshness.   It will be his cure.

BURLEIGH.

Pray, cease this wrangle.
It doth not suit the serious times in which
We live.   'Twere nobler if we set our minds
To work to save our country and our queen.
We're all like sheep within a fold.   There's in
Our midst a sly and ravenous wolf, who doth
Disturb our peace.   He hath his greedy eye
Upon our shepherd, whom he hath deceived
By conduct meek.   It is our duty, then,
To watch untiringly his movements, lest
He fall on her and ruin all.

ACT II.

SCENE I. — *Apartment in Westminster Palace.*
ELIZABETH *and* KATE ASHLEY *discovered.*

ELIZABETH.

I would that I were married, Kate.   Methinks
It is a happier life to lead than is
The solitude of barren singleness.
I oft repent me, wench, that I refused
The noble kings who would have married me.
I oft have cried myself to sleep, and then
Have dreamt of happiness, to wake again
To cold and stern reality.   Ah, Kate,
Be glad thou dost not wear a crown.   It is
A weighty ornament; yea, oftentimes
A crushing burden unto me.   I'd feel
So free if it were shared by one who had
True love for me.   But I am getting old,
I know, and have already passed the age
For men to fall in love with me.

KATE ASHLEY.

Nay, child,
Thou art not old. Thou'rt in the prime of life.
I'll warrant me no one could guess thy age,
So young and fresh thou look'st. I'll warrant me,
If thou wouldst only favour them and draw
Them on, that many young ones would be pleased
To marry thee.

ELIZABETH.

Dost think so, Kate?

KATE ASHLEY.

'Tis true.
I were most blind to question it.

ELIZABETH.

Am I good-looking, Kate?

KATE ASHLEY.

Thy beauty is much envied, child. I know
That there are many, even in this court,
Who pride themselves upon their loveliness,
But yet confess, when thou art by, thou dost
Eclipse them all. Thou'rt like the sun, which doth
Outshine the moon and stars, and pales their
    light.

ELIZABETH.

Have they confessed so much?

KATE ASHLEY.

Could they confess aught else?

ELIZABETH.

I had my charms at one time, Kate.

KATE ASHLEY.

When thou wert young no maiden in the land
Was half so beautiful.   Before thou worest
A crown thou hadst a queenly majesty.
Thou wert a picture which made glad the eye,
And thrilled the heart to gaze upon.   Thy mind
Is not less powerful and keen than is
Thy body beautiful.   Thou art the gift
Of bounteous God, who's fashioned thee a queen
Most perfectly.

ELIZABETH.

Sweet Kate!
To thee I owe a debt which I can ne'er
Repay.   Had it not been for thee, my mind
Would long ago have lost its vigour.

KATE ASHLEY.

Nay, child.
The soil in which the seeds are sown must be
Quite suitable, or else the seeds will die.

ELIZABETH.

Those were my happiest days, my wench, when I
Would sit and learn the lessons thou didst teach.
I would those happy hours would come again.
Nay, let me cast aside my cares, and let
Me be thy pupil o'er again.

KATE ASHLEY.

With all my heart.

ELIZABETH.

Now, Kate,
Let's talk of flowers. Thou know'st my love for
them
Is deep. How glorious looks this rose! Can
aught
Be lovelier?

KATE ASHLEY.

Naught, child.

ELIZABETH.

How old is it,
As thou wouldst think?

KATE ASHLEY.

But very young.

ELIZABETH.

Some years?

KATE ASHLEY.

Nay, child.
A rose's life is counted by the hours.

ELIZABETH.

To-morrow, then, 'twill be near death ?

KATE ASHLEY.

Yea.

ELIZABETH.

Like all things on this earth, true loveliness
Is only given to youth ?

KATE ASHLEY.

'Tis sadly true.

ELIZABETH.

As age creeps on that beauty fades ?

KATE ASHLEY.

True.

ELIZABETH.

How like are flowers to human beings, Kate !

KATE ASHLEY.

They're very like.

ELIZABETH.

Youth is the time of beauty, but old age
The time of ugliness ?

KATE ASHLEY.

I would it were not so.

ELIZABETH.

It is, my wench ?

KATE ASHLEY.

Yea ; it is.

ELIZABETH.

Then I am ugly, Kate, for I am old ?

KATE ASHLEY.

Nay, nay.

ELIZABETH.

Thou saidst that ugliness did come with age.

KATE ASHLEY.

I did ?

ELIZABETH.

Thou didst most solemnly.

KATE ASHLEY.

But there are cases known when nature's laws
Have been reversed. I've heard of miracles.

ELIZABETH.

But not in our time, Kate.

KATE ASHLEY.

In my time, child. Thou art a miracle.
Besides, thou art not old, but in the prime
Of life. Thou art but thirty-nine, but none
Would guess that thou wert twenty-nine.

ELIZABETH.

But thou wilt let them know my age?

KATE ASHLEY.

     Nay, never child.
I'd cut my tongue out first.

        [*Exeunt both.*

SCENE II. — *A street in London. Enter* TWO
GENTLEMEN *in conversation.*

1ST GENT.

Come, tell me what thou knowest.

2ND GENT.

There's naught to tell. The story can be told
in briefest language.

1st Gent.

But thou art far too brief, for thou dost use
no words at all.

2nd Gent.

Nay, nay. I've clothed it in the language it
doth need.

1st Gent.

Well, well, let's see. Thou saidst the queen
had quarrelled with her lover Leicester. So far
so good, but there thou stay'st. What was the
cause of it? What hath he done to raise her
ire?

2nd Gent.

How could I tell thee if I knew it not? 'Tis
known he's in disgrace, but why, 'tis known to
none.

1st Gent.

'Tis strange! Then it must be some secret
act of his.

2nd Gent.

It may have been a public one for aught the
world doth know.

1st Gent.

How doth he seem?

2ND GENT.

'Tis said he takes it very ill. It is a blow which hath quite bent his head, so now, instead of gazing at high heaven, he doth regard the earth as one that loves it.

1ST GENT.

How great a change! Methought he scorned the earth, and did despise it e'en to walk upon.

2ND GENT.

Yea, friend, our necks are frail. The strongest can't support the head for long which ever gazes at high heaven. Fatigue doth bend it down that it may rest awhile.

1ST GENT.

He'll hold it up again, I fear.

2ND GENT.

Pray God, 'tis permanently bent!

[*Exeunt* GENTLEMEN.

Enter SUSSEX *and* SIR CHRISTOPHER HATTON *in conversation.*

SUSSEX.

I tell thee, Chris, the queen is tired of him.
I'm not surprised. His arrogance would tire

And would outrage far gentler sovereigns
Than mighty Bess. I'm in a happier mood
To-day than I have been for years.

HATTON.

                    I would I were.
I greatly fear she will o'erlook his fault,
Whate'er it is, and will forgive him.

SUSSEX.

                    Ah! never fear.
Rest certain she hath done with him. I know
Her nature far too well to fear she will
Restore him to her favour. Thou couldst not
Have marked the frown with which she looked
        at him
To-day. That is a cloud which ever will
In future darken Leicester's path. Yea, more,
'Twill threaten many certain storms.

HATTON.

I would I had thy sanguine temper, Sussex.

SUSSEX.

My nature is no sanguine one, but when
I see a thing I can believe my eyes.

Enter Sir John Melville, Burleigh, *and* Lincoln.

SUSSEX.

Well met, my happy friends! Thy faces look
Most wondrous bright to-day.

MELVILLE.

Because the sun doth shine, my lord.

SUSSEX.

But not on all, Sir John.
It hath its dark side, too.   (*They laugh.*)

MELVILLE.

Thou'rt in a merry mood to-day.

SUSSEX.

There's cause for it.
Art thou not merry too?

MELVILLE.

Most merry, friend.
I would these happy times were not so rare.

SUSSEX.

That is their great defect.

Enter LEICESTER, *looking downcast. They all frown
on him.*

SUSSEX (*as he passes*).

Alas! crestfallen quite.

(LEICESTER *turns and scowls at* SUSSEX.)

LEICESTER.

There was a time when my Lord Sussex would
Have bitten out his tongue than said such words.

SUSSEX.

Liar !
When did I show that I feared thee ?

LEICESTER (*turning to the others*).

Ye all will rue this day.
[*Exit* LEICESTER.

SUSSEX.

Come, friends, let's join in feast, to celebrate
This happy day.
[*Exeunt all.*

SCENE III. — *France. A room in the Palace.
Enter* CATHERINE DE MEDICIS, *alone.*

I cannot let so fair a country slip
From out my grasp. Shall I be foiled ? Nay,
    shall
This paltry Queen of England crush my hopes ?
Shall Catherine de Medicis, the queen
Of mighty France, whom e'en the Pope doth fear,
Be conquered by a giddy girl ? Nay, God !
Thou didst not bring me in the world for that.

Thou'lt give me England yet. Thou'lt let me
    bring
So heretic a nation back to Thee,
And to Thy own true Church. Thou'lt let her be
Espoused to France and governed by those
    kings
Who are the bulwarks of the Catholic faith,
The enemies of heresy. She hath
Refused two sons of mine, whom I held out
As worthy baits. I have a younger son,
Who, though he be deformed in body, is
A worthy match for her; yea, worthy also
To rule a nation full of clowns and boors.
I'll make her marry him. I know a way
To cure her obstinacy.

        Enter KING CHARLES IX.

                Well, son?

          CHARLES.

Well, mother!

          CATHERINE.

    What means this grieving mood?

          CHARLES.

Is there not grievous cause for it?

          CATHERINE.

                Nay.

CHARLES.

Nay?

CATHERINE.

Nay, I say;
There is no grievous cause for it.

CHARLES.

Not ruinous and useless wars, whereby
We see our country's glory fade?

CATHERINE.

These things are paltry, child.

CHARLES.

Nay, do not jest.
Pray be more serious.

CATHERINE.

I am most serious.

CHARLES.

Although I know thee well, I cannot guess
What thou dost mean.

CATHERINE.

Then listen, boy.
Why need we fear our enemies when we
Have England on our side?

CHARLES.

This is but jesting.
Why, England is our greatest enemy.
'Tis she who long hath dealt us deadly blows ;
Nay, but for her all Europe would be ours.

CATHERINE.

We'll conquer Europe yet,
And England shall assist us.

CHARLES.

Nay, mother,
Thou knowst there is no ground for such high
hopes.

CATHERINE.

I have a son that shall rule England yet !

CHARLES.

Pray how ?

CATHERINE.

Elizabeth shall be his wife.

CHARLES.

Which son ?

CATHERINE.

Thy brother, Alençon.

CHARLES.

She'll never wed so ill-deformed a man.
She hath refused to marry handsome men,
Most powerful kings, and I am certain she
Would scorn an ill-assorted match. Nay, more,
She'd feel insulted, and would seek revenge.
'Twould bring a greater breach between us, which
No effort on our part would ever bridge.
It cannot be.

CATHERINE.

I say it shall be.
She need not know of his great ugliness.
If there are any likely to impart
To her the truth, then gold can silence them.
Nay, more, it shall be made to hide thy brother's
Deformity, and make him look a man
Of handsome and attractive form. Ah, gold
Will tinsel o'er and change to brilliancy
The coarsest things. On it I will rely
For sure success.

CHARLES.

The secret will leak out, and we are damned.

CATHERINE.

'Tis worth the trial, thou'lt confess, and if
It fails there's naught will damn us, son.

CHARLES.

I'll leave it all to thee.
Thou art a clever woman, far too deep
For man to fathom thee, or woman, either.
Thou hast done wondrous things ere now, and
    hast,
No doubt, the faculty to do them still.

CATHERINE.

I have the will
To do what nature can.   I cannot suffer
Defeat from anyone, and least of all
From woman.

              [Exeunt both.

SCENE IV.—*London.   An apartment in the Queen's
Palace.*

Enter ELIZABETH *and* BURLEIGH.

ELIZABETH.

Nay, Cecil, urge me not.   I cannot steel
My heart to murder her.

BURLEIGH.

'Twould not be murder, but a prudent act.
Nay, justice would be met by it, and thou
Hast great desire to be just.   Ye must

Put Mary, Queen of Scots, to death, or else
Thou'lt ne'er know peace.

ELIZABETH.

I'd know no peace if I lopped off her head.
I cannot, my Lord Burleigh, give consent,
So let it rest.

BURLEIGH.

It is for love of thee I urge thee thus;
It is the love I bear my country that
Dictates my counsel, gracious majesty.
I would not see thee killed, my country robbed
Of such a wise and virtuous queen, and ruled
By blood-stained murderers, the enemies
Of God and man. If thou wilt have no thought
For thine own self, think of thy subjects' grief
If they should lose so good a queen. They
    know
Thy life is placed in jeopardy, and this
Doth cause them poignant sorrow, such as thou
Canst not conceive. They use my mouth to
    speak
Their inward thoughts, and their one prayer is
    this—
That thou wilt put to most deservéd death
This Mary, Queen of Scots.

ELIZABETH.

Ah, Cecil, well I know thy heart, and thy
Great love for me. Thou art an honest man,
And wise, but thou art liable to err.
Methinks thy judgment's gone astray for once.
I see no danger if she lives. She's safe
Imprisoned in a castle, whence escape
Is difficult ; nay, more, impossible.
How can a queen of feeble health, in such
A place, and watched with eagle eyes,
Concoct a plot to murder me ? 'Twould be
A miracle, thou must confess. What use
A captive bird, whose wings are clipped, to sigh
For liberty, if when the door was oped
It fell unto the ground ? 'Twere safer in
The cage, for there it would not run the risk
Of being trampled on. Thou hast my word.
I am resolved to let her live. She's not
So bad as thou wouldst make her out.

BURLEIGH.

The captive bird hath friends. 'Tis they whom
    thou
Must fear. Their love for her hath bred deep
    hate
To thee. They're not confined. Their minds
    and hands

Are free, and they would die, and count it glory,
To aid her cause. It, then, is natural
That they should plot to murder thee, and place
The one they love upon the throne. If she
Were dead they'd risk their lives in vain.

ELIZABETH.

I have decided, my good lord.

[*Exit* BURLEIGH.

An honest and a worthy man, whose zeal
Hath blinded him. He cannot see I've not
The heart to sign the warrant for her death.
It is a task beyond my courage. I know
Whilst she doth live my life's in jeopardy,
And yet I am not bold enough to make
It safe, or to remove the magazine
On which my throne is set. But need I fear
Whilst it is watched so zealously and with
Such loving eyes as Burleigh has? I know
He'll guard me well. Ah! would I had
Around my throne more like my lord. My throne
Would then be placed upon a mighty rock,
Which storms could never shake. But I must be
The tool of hypocrites! God's death! I know
Their faces well. I'll sift the chaff and find
A worthy storehouse for it, too.

Enter LEICESTER.

(*The Queen does not see him. He approaches her and kneels at her feet, his forehead bowed to the ground. She suddenly sees him.*)

ELIZABETH.

What beast is crawling here?

LEICESTER.

No beast, beloved majesty, but one
Who's nearly dead with grief, who's come to sue
For life.

ELIZABETH.

To sue for that which thou dost not deserve?
Thou shouldst be grateful thou dost live, and
    hast
The strength to crawl. But crawl not here;
    this is
No place for worms. I have a place beside
The Thames will suit thee best.

LEICESTER.

Nay, mighty queen, most gracious majesty,
The world itself is like the Tower to me.
It is a prison where I never see
The sun which gladdens all. Thou wert my sun,
But since thy light was hid from me I've lived
In gloom. Pray, pity me, for whom thou hadst

4

A love which others did not share.   It is
To me a grievous punishment to know
That I have lost that love, but if thou hidest
Thy face from me 'twill be my death.

ELIZABETH.

Well, thou wert better dead.

LEICESTER.

O God !

And canst thou not be merciful ?

ELIZABETH.

Be merciful to thee ?
Hast thou shown mercy unto me ?

LEICESTER.

I do confess, most gracious majesty,
That I have erred and have offended thee.
But wilt thou not forgive ?   Thou hast forgiven
Far deeper crimes than mine, not done in love
For thee, as mine.   I crave not for thy love—
For I have forfeited what's so divine—
But for forgiveness.   Let me plead my love.
'Twas that that urged my tongue to utter forth
In madness feelings that were natural.
Yea, natural, for thou didst give me hope
That thou wouldst marry me.

ELIZABETH.

                    I gave thee hope?
Thou liest, hypocrite. 'Tis true I had
Much love for thee, because I thought thou wert
A man. But I have found thee out. Thou art
A base, deceitful wretch, a crawling worm.
I'd tread on thee if I were merciful,
For thou deservest death. Pray, go, vile beast,
Nor let thy presence torture me. I'll let
Thee live, but if I see thy face again,
I'll put thee in a den thou wilt not like,
But which will suit thy nature well.

(*Exit* LEICESTER, *crestfallen.* ELIZABETH, *after
his departure, is for some moments silent.*)

O that I could recall such bitter words!
Too late! too late! They've deeply wounded
      him.
Poor Leicester! thou wilt suffer agony,
And I the cause of it! I do repent.
I am to blame. I am too hard of heart.
I know thy love for me is deep and true,
And I've repaid it with ingratitude
And angry words. 'Tis I who need forgiveness.
Thy grief will give me rest nor day nor night.

O would I had a softer heart ! I then
Would know——

(La Motte Fénelon *is announced.*)

Monsieur is welcome here.

Fénelon.

I thank thee, great and mighty queen. I feel
Most honoured by thy graciousness.

Elizabeth.

What would my lord ambassador ?

Fénelon.

To tell your majesty the happy news,
The Queen of France, the wife of good King
    Charles,
Hath borne a daughter.

Elizabeth.

           A daughter ?
Methought it was a son.

Fénelon.

The rumour spread abroad it was a son,
But it was false.

Elizabeth.

        I send them greetings.
Go, write unto the noble king and queen

That I rejoice with them.   The little princess
Will be most welcomed in the world.   I pray
That God may give her joy and happiness
Proportioned to her rank and high descent.

FÉNELON.

I will convey such kind and gracious words
To those who'll be most touched by them.

[*Exit* FÉNELON.

ELIZABETH.

How every hour events do hap to tell,
In blatant tones, that I'm a barren stock !
That I'm alone, and have not e'en a child
To love me and to ease, with prattling talk,
My weighty cares !   I'm called on to rejoice
With others when they have the sweet delights
Denied to me.   What mockery !   O God,
What hollowness !   They little know the pain
Such greetings give to me.   Fierce jealousy
Doth seem to gnaw my heart and make me hate
Such happy mortals.   Oh, I envy them ;
I envy all, both high and low, who know
What children's love is like.   I've tasted all
The pleasures of this world but that of love.
Who loves me ?   They who do pretend a love
Do hate me in their hearts, for love assumed
Is hatred in disguise.   They know 'tis well

To humour me.   Their welfare doth depend
On pleasing me.   Dependence is the soil
Most fertile for the growth of hate, and that's
The soil in which my life is cast.   I am
The most unenviable of queens.

> [*Exit* ELIZABETH.

SCENE V.—*Night.   A country place.*

Enter LEICESTER *and* COUNTESS OF ESSEX.

COUNTESS OF ESSEX.

Methinks thou art a deep and wondrous man.
The queen is angered, and thy enemies
Rejoice o'er thy discomfiture, and boast
They'll bring thee further down.   Thy hopes
And thy ambition have received a blow,
Enough to crush thee, yet thou wear'st a smile,
And art most light of heart; nay, full of joy.
Thou rather shouldst be in a grievous mood,
As other men would be.

LEICESTER.

                    Ha! ha!
Thou dost not know me yet.   'Twere time thou
    didst,
For I am easily read.

COUNTESS OF ESSEX.

Thou'rt not indeed.
Thy character is writ in language which
Requires no common skill to read.

LEICESTER.

Nay, is it so?
Then I may pride myself on this?

COUNTESS OF ESSEX.

Thou mayst indeed.

LEICESTER.

My character is rare, thou sayst?

COUNTESS OF ESSEX.

'Tis very rare.

LEICESTER.

I'm glad on it.

COUNTESS OF ESSEX.

Glad!

LEICESTER.

Ay, glad.

COUNTESS OF ESSEX.

Pray why?

LEICESTER.

Dost think I'd have a common nature, love?
My great ambition is to be—pray, guess.

COUNTESS OF ESSEX.

I am no skilful guesser ; 'tis, no doubt,
As strange as is thyself.

LEICESTER.

            It is, I must confess,
But 'tis no foolish one, but one most wise.
It is to be unlike the common kind
In everything.   I wish to stand aloof,
To be above them, out of reach of them.
They know my handsome form doth make them
      look
Contemptible and mean, and doth attract
The favour of the queen.   This angers them,
As is most natural.   I knew not I
Possessed so many gifts until this hour.
Thy words have cured my sorrow and have fed
My heart with hope, for which I thank thee,
      sweet.

COUNTESS OF ESSEX.

Then is it I who've filled thee with this joy?

LEICESTER.

'Tis thou !
And is it not most natural ?   To whom
Should I, in sorrow, look for sympathy
But thee ?   Thou art the source of all my joy.
Thou art the light which dissipates the gloom
In which my life is ofttimes cast.   Thou art
The sun for which I look in certain hope
Through long and tedious nights.   It would be
    strange
If thou shouldst bring me grief, or make me live
In deeper gloom, or make my life but one
Perpetual night.

COUNTESS OF ESSEX.

Doth it increase thy love for me ?

LEICESTER.

My love for thee !
I cannot measure it ; it reaches heights
So lofty, and extends to depths profound.
The more I see of thee, the more I hear
Thy heavenly voice, the more I contemplate
Thy wondrous loveliness, the more my love
Doth grow, and my desire to wed thee soon.
But list !   Who comes this way ?   Canst thou
    not hear ?

COUNTESS OF ESSEX.

The tones are harsh and fierce.

LEICESTER.

Come, let's conceal ourselves behind yon hedge ;
'Twere best we were not seen.

[LEICESTER *and* COUNTESS OF ESSEX *retire.*

Enter LADY MOLE (*late* FREEZE) *and her husband,*
SIR THOMAS MOLE.

MOLE.

Oh that I had not married thee !   Had I
Been keen of sight, I would have seen and steered
With safety past the iceberg which hath wrecked
My life.

LADY MOLE.

But what of me,
Thou heartless, godless, and abandoned wretch ?
Where hast thou guided me ?   To what a place
Have I been brought !   O perfect misery !
Away from light, from loveliness, and all
That's dear on earth, to dirt, and gloom, and all
That is repellent to pure taste.

MOLE.

Pure taste, indeed !
Is it pure taste that forms such ugly words

As thou dost utter forth ?   Is it pure taste
That makes thee bawl and shout, that makes thee
    strive
To be a thing inhuman ?   I thought pure taste
Was that which loved a quiet, happy life,
And not a cold and dull, repulsive one.

LADY MOLE.

I utter ugly words ?   I bawl and shout ?
Yea, I a thing inhuman ?   What art thou ?
Yea, what must thou be with thy filth and dirt ?
What language could describe thee truthfully ?
Thou sayst my life is cold and dull.   Who's made
It so ?   Who's kept from me the warmth and
    light ?
Who's brought me this unhappiness ?   Yea, who
Hath dragged me down to misery ?   'Tis thou !
'Tis thou, I say !   Thou cold and heartless man !
Thou fiend, worse than the devil himself !

MOLE.

                              Ha, ha !
Yea, I'm to blame !   I've brought thee all this
    grief !
I've been a cruel husband !   Yea, thou dost
Deserve much sympathy.   Henceforth I'll try
To be as kind and gentle unto thee
As was thy former husband, whom ye killed.

Poor man! I pity him! His end was sad,
To leave a wife so loving.

LADY MOLE.

What!

Am I a murderess? O God, what next!
What will this wicked man accuse me of?
Oh, wilt Thou let him live and say such things?
Such lies? What punishment doth he deserve?
Is there on earth his equal—one so vile?
As full of wickedness and all disease
As grapes of honeyed juice! O wretched me!
Oh, think of it, that I'm to live with him!
O days of darkness yet to come! O woe!
O perfect wretchedness! Oh, pity me,
A poor defenceless woman, who dost stand
In need of sympathy and help!

MOLE.

Thou need'st not stand in need of it. Thou
    need'st
Not call for sympathy and help. Thou need'st
Not live with me. I'd gladly let thee go,
Where'er thou wilt, that I might live in peace.

LADY MOLE.

That doth betray thee well—thy cruel heart.
Thou wouldst abandon me and let me face,
Alone, the cheerless world.

MOLE.

That would not be a new experience ;
For thou wert facing it courageously
Before I married thee.

LADY MOLE.

O wretch !
Whate'er I say thou tripp'st me up.   I'll speak
My thoughts no more, but act them out.
[Exeunt both.

Re-enter LEICESTER *and* COUNTESS OF ESSEX.

COUNTESS OF ESSEX.

And dost thou know them, love ?

LEICESTER.

I know them well.
Such scenes as these were prophesied before
They wed.   I do not pity him, for he
Would marry her in spite of sage advice.
He had no lack of friends who warned him well,
And would have saved him from this wreck.   I
    could
Recount to thee the story of her life.
'Tis full of interest, though not of acts
Deserving praise.   It's been a varied life,
Where virtue's had but little sway.   'Tis true,

And is well known, her former husband died
Not from excessive love.   Couldst thou, my sweet,
Be such a wife to me ?

COUNTESS OF ESSEX.

Nay, Dudley,
Thou know'st my love for thee is much too deep
And true.   I pity him.   I think he is
Deserving sympathy.

LEICESTER.

Nay, let's dismiss all thoughts of both, and talk
Of our own joys and of the happiness
That is to be when we are man and wife.

COUNTESS OF ESSEX.

I'd rather think of them awhile, and of
The lives they lead.   I feel quite sad.

LEICESTER.

Come, come !
I cannot let thee brood o'er this.   Forget
This scene, and bend thy thoughts on me and on
The time when I shall marry thee.

[*Exeunt both.*

SCENE VI.—*France. A garden at the Royal Castle of Blois. Enter* CATHERINE DE MEDICIS SIR THOMAS SMITH (*a very short man*), *and* WALSINGHAM.

CATHERINE.

I have great sympathy for her indeed.
She's in the midst of scheming enemies,
Who seek her ruin.   She is not safe, alone.
It is not natural that she should guide,
Alone, a ship so great, and carrying
Such precious souls.   It is a treacherous sea
O'er which her voyage lies.   No woman's strength
Could battle with success the fearful storms
That constantly and suddenly arise.
She needs a captain, bold, experienced,
In whom she may, with safety, put her trust.

WALSINGHAM.
                'Tis very true.
I would that she relied less on herself.

SMITH.

Nay, if she had a captain, she would want
To guide the ship herself.

WALSINGHAM.
                Yea, 'tis very true.

CATHERINE.

But if he were a skilful man, he would
Refuse to let her guide.   Though she might bawl,
It need not loosen his firm hold.   There is
A way of doing this with gentleness.

WALSINGHAM.

                              Ay, true !

SMITH.

I'd dare to argue thus with her—and will !

CATHERINE.

                              Nay, wilt thou ?

SMITH.

I will, by God !

CATHERINE.

Thou art most brave.   I do admire thee.
I see thou lov'st thy country and thy queen.

SMITH.

                    Most fervently.
I'd sell my life to save them both.

WALSINGHAM.

Nor would I hesitate to lay down mine.

CATHERINE.

Ye both are worthy, noble men.   I would
Such men were grown in France.   Alas, we have
Too few !   Is Norfolk executed yet ?

WALSINGHAM.
Nay,
Not that we have learnt.

CATHERINE.

Belike the queen will pardon him ?

WALSINGHAM.
We cannot tell.

CATHERINE.

I would that she were quiet from these broils.

BOTH.
I would she were.

CATHERINE.

She could be if she chose.

BOTH.
Pray, how ?

CATHERINE.

By marrying.

5

SMITH.

'Twere well if she would wed.

CATHERINE.

Dost think that she could fancy marriage with
My son, the Duc d'Alençon ?

SMITH.

Madam,
Thou knowest me of old. Except I have
A certain ground, I dare not say how she
Would act in such a case.

WALSINGHAM.

No man could tell her mind on this.

CATHERINE.

Come, tell me, do ye think yourselves that she
Could marry one more worthy her ? Though I
May justly be considered partial to
My son, yet I have heard it stated that
The emperor's son, the Archduke Rodolf, or
E'en John of Austria, are not so noble,
But much inferior to Alençon.

BOTH.

We do not doubt it, madam.

CATHERINE.

If your most gracious majesty intends
To wed, it were a pity much more time
Was lost.

SMITH.

We know not that she doth intend to wed.
If it pleased God she married and did have
A child, these brags and treasons would be soon
Appeased, and if its father were thy son,
The duke, I would not care, so long as she
Were guarded well and safe.

CATHERINE.

I would that it were done, for I would then
Go o'er and see her, which I much desire.

SMITH.

Yea, if I had
As ample a commission now as I
Once had for Monsieur le Duc d'Anjou,
The thing would soon be at an end.

CATHERINE.

Oh, would thou hadst !
Yea, if thou hadst another one, on thy
Return to England wouldst thou come to France
Again to execute it ?

SMITH.

Yea, madam,
Most gladly.   For so good a purpose would
I cross the sea again, if I were never
So sick.

WALSINGHAM.

I would be glad to lend my aid in what
I so desire, and which I think would be
For our best good.

CATHERINE.

I'm glad on it.
I hope she will commission ye.

BOTH.

I hope so, madam.

SMITH.

If she were wed, all trait'rous hearts would be
Discouraged, for one tree alone is soon
Cut down, but two or three together take
Much longer doing.

CATHERINE.

I see no reason why the queen should not
Have many children.

SMITH.

I would to God that she had one.

WALSINGHAM.

Amen !

CATHERINE.

Nay, two boys, lest the one should die.

SMITH.

Thou thinkst the duke would speed ?

CATHERINE (*laughing*).

Je le désire infinitement.
I doubt, howe'er, he will not grow so tall
As is his brother, le Duc d'Anjou.
He is not short, indeed, for he's as tall
As thou.

SMITH.

That cannot be an obstacle. I make
But small account of that, indeed. I have
No admiration for tall men, for did
Not Pepin bring forth Charlemagne, though he
Scarce reached the girdle of his wife ? And then
Your Oliver, the Breton constable,
According to his tomb he must have been
But four feet high, and yet ye worship him
For his great deeds. He was a valiant man,
And dreaded most by Englishmen. The duke's
Short stature's not the thing that thou need'st
   dread.

CATHERINE.

I'm glad on it.
Perchance thou'lt bring it yet to pass.

SMITH.

We'll try,
And have great hopes we shall succeed.

CATHERINE.

Pray God ye will.

BOTH.

Amen.
[*Exeunt* SMITH *and* WALSINGHAM.

CATHERINE.

My bark is sailing with a fav'ring wind.
I see fair weather for some time to come.
These silly men assist me on my course,
Because they think I'll bring them to a place
Where's found prosperity. They little know
The shoals and sands which they will meet, nor
    see
The rock on which they will be wrecked. Ha!
    ha!
I'm prospering beyond my fondest hopes.
Ah, proud, conceited queen, I'll humble thee!
I'll tumble thee from that proud eminence

Where thou hast set thyself! My hate for thee
Is such that time will ne'er appease it, nor
Submission soften it. I know a way
To kill thee out, but I prefer to see
Thy ling'ring agony. That is a joy
I shall experience ere long.

Enter the Duc d'Alençon.

ALENÇON.

I see thou'rt happy, mother.

CATHERINE.

And thou hast need to be, my son. These men
Are safe. They'll urge the marriage on. I know
The queen doth put great trust in them, and will
Be guided by their counsel; so thou need'st
Must live in hope thou wilt rule England yet.
Thou know'st the purport of our talk?

ALENÇON.

                I heard it all,
And marked how well ye managed it and led
Them on. I'm proud of thee.

CATHERINE.

             And thou hast need to be.
To me alone thou'lt owe the fortune which
Has been denied to others worthier it.

Howe'er, this is not yet success.   There's much
To do and much to reason out.

ALENÇON.

But naught too difficult for thee.

CATHERINE.

God knows, my son.
[*Exeunt* CATHERINE *and* ALENÇON.

ACT III.

SCENE I.—*London. An apartment in the Palace at Westminster.*

Enter QUEEN ELIZABETH *reading a letter from the* DUC D'ALENÇON.

' To the beautiful and virtuous Queen of England.

' MOST ESTEEMED MAJESTY,

'O that I had words that could befittingly express my thoughts! Alas! I can but feebly write them. O that I could see thy own true self, my eyes, my every organ would utter forth and emphasize the truth of what my heart doth wish to say. I live in hopes, beloved and most gracious majesty, that thou wilt look on me as one who doth deserve to look on thee ; to come quite close to thee ; yea, say the words which love alone inspires. I've heard men speak of thee as one most wondrous fair; divinely virtuous ;

possessing wisdom that befits thy mighty rank. My heart doth prompt me, yea, compels me to adore and worship thee ; to love thee ; for thou'rt worthy of the love of any king or prince. Pray let me offer at thy virgin shrine my humble self, as one who would aspire to marry thee and cherish thee with fervent and undying love.

‘ Devoutly kneeling, I salute with gratitude thy beauteous hand, and live in hope thou'lt favour me.

    ‘ Thy humble, faithful servant,

        ‘ ALENÇON.’

ELIZABETH.

The words are sweetly beautiful.   Methinks
He is a noble and a virtuous prince,
Yea, far above my suitors hitherto.
Their language was as coarse as was their love,
Their sentiments as harsh, as dull, as cold,
But here I cannot find a fault.   The words
Are perfect, full of sweetness, grace, and truth.
Could any coarse soul utter them ?   Yea, could
A man who had no loving, noble heart
Express such lovely thoughts ?   Could sweetness
    come
From what is sour ?   Could flowers spring up in
    soil

That is not favourable to their growth ? Nay,
    nay.
Could loveliness spring forth from barrenness ?
Could wisdom speak the words of ignorance ?
Could nature change her laws and be untrue ?
This prince doth please me well. I like his
    thoughts
And words, and I am sure shall like himself.

Enter La Motte Fénelon.

FÉNELON.

Good-morrow, gracious majesty !

ELIZABETH.

               Good-morrow, Fénelon.
What wills my lord ambassador ?

FÉNELON.

To pay my true respects unto your majesty.

ELIZABETH.

                    Ha !
Thy countenance doth speak another object.
Pray, out with it, for I do hate delay.

FÉNELON.

Thy marvellous gifts have truly read my face.
Thou hast an insight into human looks
Most wonderful, yet quite consistent with

Thy other matchless gifts.   Then thus it is.
I would that thou couldst give an answer to
My master's gracious message unto thee.

ELIZABETH.

                         So soon ?   What !
No time to think it o'er ?   Come, Fénelon,
Thou art not serious !   This is a matter
Which should take years to think upon.   Dost thou
Not know a virgin's heart ?   What ! wouldst thou have
A woman give her heart to any man,
When he doth ask for it, without a thought
Of what she doth ?   How longer should she think,
How exercise more prudence, when she is
A queen ?   She studies not herself alone,
Nor her own heart.   It is her subjects' heart,
And their souls' welfare which she gives away ;
And thou dost seek a speedy answer !   Fie !
I thought thou wert a more considerate man.

FÉNELON.

Forgive me, gracious majesty, if I
Have been o'er-hasty.   I plead the strong excuse
Of my poor master's love for thee.   Pray, think
Of him, and all the pangs delay will bring

To him. 'Tis natural his mighty love
Should pine for words of hope. It is the food
For which he's hungering. I love him so,
I would not have him starve and pine, when thou
Couldst feed him up with angels' food.

ELIZABETH.

I doubt he hath this love for me.

FÉNELON.

What !
Canst doubt his love ? O God, would all could
    love
As he ! Who could not love thee ?

ELIZABETH.

I've had no proofs of it.

FÉNELON.

No proofs !
I thought thou wert o'erwhelmed with proofs.

ELIZABETH.

A written letter is no proof.

FÉNELON.

I grant it ; yea,
I grant it, but I've in my keep a proof

Which must convince thee, or thou ne'er wilt be
Convinced.

ELIZABETH.

What is it, pray?

FÉNELON.

A letter which he wrote some years ago
Unto his bosom friend, De Foix.   I found
This letter 'mongst the papers of his friend,
And though I've no commands to show it thee,
I'll let thee read it if thou hast a wish.

ELIZABETH.

With all my heart,
And hope I'll find in it the proof I need.

FÉNELON (*handing the letter*).

Pray God thou wilt.

ELIZABETH (*reads*).

'I echo fervently what thou dost say.   From
all reports she is an angel, though in human form.
I count it happiness to worship such a one.   How
happy must that nation be whose queen she is!
But, oh, how blest and happy must that mortal
be to whom she gives a wifely love!   I'd tell her
of my love if I could hope she'd deign to marry

me. But no! It cannot be. I was not born
for such great happiness. She's worthy of a
greater and a nobler one. I must content myself with love and admiration from afar.

> 'Thy everlasting friend,
>
> > 'ALENÇON.'

I must confess 'tis written well.

FÉNELON.

But wilt thou not confess
It is a proof of his undying love?

ELIZABETH.

I do not doubt his love,
But my own worthiness to be the wife
Of such a noble prince. For I am old,
And he is young, and after we've been wed
A little time he will despise me.

FÉNELON.

Nay, canst thou doubt thy worth? Thou dost
thyself
A grievous wrong. It is the duke who is
Unworthy thee. Nay, as for age, there's no
Disparity in that. The difference
Is but the trifling one of nineteen years,
And as thy charms of person and of mind

Make thee look younger by ten years, and as
The manly figure, wisdom, and good grace
Of monsieur doth make him look more aged by
　　full
Nine years, ye're on equality.

Enter LEICESTER.

But I will leave thee, gracious majesty,
And live in hopes thou'lt know thy charms,
And be less humble.
　　　　　　[*Exit* FÉNELON, *scowling at* LEICESTER.

ELIZABETH.

What dost thou here?

LEICESTER.

To be in the sun.

ELIZABETH.

But clouds are coming on.

LEICESTER.

　　　　　　Nay, gracious majesty;
I hope thou ne'er wilt frown on me again.
'Twill be my death.

ELIZABETH.

　　　　　　Poor man!
I've acted cruelly to thee.

LEICESTER.

Nay, thou hast ever been most kind.

ELIZABETH.

Thou hast deserved my smiles.

LEICESTER.

I have deserved thy censure, thou dost mean.

ELIZABETH.

Nay, Leicester, thou hast served me faithfully.
Thy love for me hath been the only love
On which I could rely. Those who pretend
To worship me, who make the most parade
Of their great love, are cringing hypocrites.
They think I cannot read their lying hearts,
But I'll translate their words some day
To their discomfiture. How happy should
I feel if all my subjects were as true,
As loving, and sincere as thou! But no;
There's but one Leicester in the land, and thou
Art he.

LEICESTER.

I am not worthy of this flattery.
I have but done my duty to my queen,
As I do hope all have.

6

ELIZABETH.

But they have not, as thou well know'st, and I'm
Resolved to let them reap the fruit for which
They've sown.   They flatter me and say I'm wise,
And fit to be their queen, but in their hearts
They wish me dead, that they might have a king.

LEICESTER.

I little thought they were so false.

ELIZABETH.

Canst thou deny it ?

LEICESTER.

Thou knowest them more deeply than myself;
Long time I have suspected them.

ELIZABETH.

Hast thou had cause for it ?

LEICESTER.

I must confess I have.

ELIZABETH.

If in my youth they thought not well of me,
What must they think of me when old ?   They'll
    wish
More eagerly to have a king.

LEICESTER.

Methinks they will.

ELIZABETH.

O God!
Wouldst Thou would keep old age from me,
And let me be avenged on them! For are
They not Thine enemies as well as mine,
To spurn Thine own anointed one? But with
Thy help I will defeat them yet. I'll wed,
And let them have a king. Yea, they
Shall have their wish fulfilled, but it shall be
To their most bitter grief. I'll marry him
Who loves me for myself, that he may be
The instrument I'll use to torture them.

LEICESTER.

This were a prudent step to take, and I
Commend thee in this wise resolve.

ELIZABETH.

Wouldst thou approve of this?

LEICESTER.

There's naught on earth would please me more.

ELIZABETH.

And dost thou think it would be wise?

LEICESTER.

    I'm sure on it.

ELIZABETH.

I'll marry then, by God!

LEICESTER.

    But whom?—but when?

ELIZABETH.

As speedily as matters will allow.

LEICESTER.

But thou hast spurned thy suitors and hast none
Possessing qualities thou canst admire.

ELIZABETH.

    Nay, Dudley, nay.
I know there's one on earth who hath a love
For me too deep to be untrue; who hath
A noble nature, too.

LEICESTER.

I would that I could guess his name.

ELIZABETH.

I'll tell it thee ere many days are o'er.

               [*Exeunt both.*

SCENE II.—*A street in London.*

Enter TWO GENTLEMEN *in conversation.*

IST GENT.

I hear that my lord Leicester is very much with her majesty, and that she shows him the great affection she was wont.

2ND GENT.

I cannot understand her, friend. She is quite beyond my skill to fathom her.

IST GENT.

She's beyond the skill of any man. I've long ceased to be surprised at anything she does, and am quite calm conversing of her freaks. Not only doth she regard him with the same liking as of yore, but tries to please him more.

2ND GENT.

Each day exhibits some new strangeness in her.

IST GENT.

They say that his enemies are greatly disconcerted, and strive in every way to grow into his liking.

2ND GENT.

Theirs is a hard and grievous task. I'd rather live in humble circumstances, friend, than be dependent on the treacherous smiles of royalty. 'Tis climbing up a steep and slippery hill. Though we may tread most carefully, we may dislodge some obstacle which lets us down to ruin. An humble life is built on firmer ground, and happiness is often hidden in security. At least, it gives more peace of mind.

1ST GENT.

Alas! these climbing men know little peace of mind. Their lot is sad, their lives are most precarious; nor do I envy them. Thou said'st the queen would pass this way?

2ND GENT.

I said so, friend. These decorations are in honour of her journey through. With what a fondness all regard her! They worship her as though she were an angel sent from heaven.

1ST GENT.

Their love for her is very deep.

2ND GENT.

Pray look at them. No sad and rueful face among them all, but beaming o'er with happiness and joy. How eagerly they wait her coming! She'll smile on them, and that will be an antidote for all their sorrows for some years to come. (*Trumpets sound.*) She comes! Let's stand aside and watch her pass.

(*Presently enter procession amidst the applause of the populace. At length enters* ELIZABETH, *with* LEICESTER, *as Master of Horse, close behind, and all other officers and dignitaries of the State.*)

CITIZENS.

God bless your gracious majesty!
Long live our blessed queen!

1ST CITIZEN.

How beautiful she looks!

2ND CITIZEN.

How graciously she bends to all and smiles!

CITIZENS.

May God preserve your majesty!
(ELIZABETH *stays the procession.*)

1ST CITIZEN.

She'll speak to us.

2ND CITIZEN.

She beckons silence, friend.

3RD CITIZEN.

Pray, silence for our gracious queen !

CITIZENS.

Silence ! silence !
The queen would speak to us.

ELIZABETH.

My loving subjects,
I thank ye all.   I see ye love me well.

(*Affirmative murmurs.*)

I'm not deserving of such honest love.

CITIZENS.

Yea, yea !
Our lives are thine, most gracious sovereign.

ELIZABETH.

My life is thine.   'Tis at your service, friends.
Command, and I will do.   If I have done
Aught ill to ye, I ask forgiveness now.
'Twas done in ignorance of what ye wish,

And I have been deceived.   I swear to make
Amends if I have done ye harm.

CITIZENS.

Thou hast not done a single subject harm,
Thou art too kind and good.

ELIZABETH.

'Tis God who hath directed me, and Him
Ye all must thank.

CITIZENS.

     We will, we will !
We'll thank Him, for He sent thee unto us.

ELIZABETH.

     'Tis true, my loving friends.
He placed me on the throne of this great land.
He sent me here to be your queen and friend,
To save ye from your enemies and His.
Yea, ye have foes amongst ye here who would
Destroy the Church and throne.   But these are
  safe,
For they are built upon your jealous love
And piety, foundations which no storm of heresy
Can overturn.   Ye're prosperous indeed,
Because ye serve and do the will of God.
I'm happy in such subjects, for I know
As long as ye are His your souls are safe,

The end for which I hourly pray.
God bless ye, friends.   I leave ye in His keeping.

(*The procession moves off amidst the enthusiasm and
applause of the populace, who run after it.   The
Two Gentlemen come forward.*)

1st Gent.

Methinks she is a godly queen.

2nd Gent.

Her thoughts were clothed most piously.   Alas!
I have a doubt of their sincerity.

1st Gent.

I have no doubt of any kind.   I look
On wonders now as things quite natural.

[*Exeunt* Two Gentlemen.

SCENE III.—*A room in the house of* Sir Christopher Hatton.

Enter Hatton *and his servant* Whitley.

Hatton.

Ah, Whitley, thou art happier than I.

Whitley.

How so, my master?   That can never be.
When thou dost grieve, I suffer pain; when thou
Art joyous, then I know true happiness.

HATTON.

Thy love for me, I know, is very deep,
But yet it cannot feel the painful stab
Which the ingratitude of queens may give.
That is reserved for me. Yea, I alone
Must suffer that keen agony.

WHITLEY.

Alas! I suffer thy ingratitude,
Which is a grievous pang to me. But yet
I know thou lov'st me well, and dost not mean
To doubt my love.

HATTON.

Nay, Whitley, nay.
I am as sure of thy great love for me
As I am of the queen's ingratitude.
There was a time when I was all in all
To her, and when she called me her sweet lids,
Her sheep, her mutton, and her belwether;
But those bright days are gone. The glorious sun
Of her sweet face is now obscured by clouds.
Alas! what ruinous and threat'ning clouds!
I fear I ne'er shall look on her again,
Or kiss her loving hand. Oh that I could!
There is some comfort, Whitley, that she writes
To me. It doth in manner ease my grief.

WHITLEY.

I would my master would forget her.

HATTON.

Forget her, Whitley! Nay, upon my life
I could not banish her.

WHITLEY.

But if thou couldst, 'twould bring more peace to
thee.

HATTON.

More peace!
Alas, poor man! I parted with it long
Ago. I ne'er shall look for peace until
I die. I'd rather think of her, in spite
Of her ingratitude, than never gaze
In meditation on her angel face.
Methinks I'll write to her.

WHITLEY.

I would not; yea, I would not.

HATTON.

Pray, why?

WHITLEY.

'Twould give her cause for mirth.

HATTON.

Nay; rather would it move her heart to pity.

WHITLEY.

Thou canst not move a stony heart with words;
But if thou couldst, what wouldst thou get from it?
Naught sweet and nourishing.

HATTON.

　　　　　She hath no stony heart.

WHITLEY.

Methinks she hath, indeed.　To thee she owes
More than she ever could repay, and yet
She spurns thee off to nurse this viper Leicester.

HATTON.

'Tis not her fault.　He hath a witch's charm,
'Gainst which the queen is powerless.　Nay,
　　Whitley,
We must not censure her, but rather should
We pity her.　I'll write to her.

WHITLEY.

But thou wilt do it 'gainst my wish.

HATTON.

　　　　　I must.
'Twill ease my mind a deal.

WHITLEY.

Well, if thou must, thou must. I say again,
Thou wilt repent it.

HATTON.

My heart constraineth me to write. (*He writes.*)

'MY MOST ESTEEMED AND GRACIOUS LADY,

'If I could express my feelings of your
gracious letters, I should utter unto you matter
of strange effect. In reading of them, with my
tears I blot them; in thinking of them, I feel so
great comfort that I find cause, God knoweth, to
read them on my knees. Madam, I find the
greatest lack that ever poor wretch sustained. I
lack *that* I live by. My spirit and soul, I feel,
agreeth with my body and life that to serve thee
is a heaven, but to lack thee is more than hell's
torment unto them. My heart is full of woe.
Pardon my tedious writing; it doth much diminish
my great griefs. Would God I were with you but
for one hour! My wits are overwrought with
thoughts. I find myself amazed. Bear with me,
my most dear, sweet lady. Passion overcometh
me. Shall I utter this dismal word, "Farewell"?
Yea, ten thousand, thousand farewells! He
speaketh it that most dearly loveth you. I hold

you too long.   Once again I crave pardon, and so
bid your own poor " lids " farewell.

> ' Your bondsman, everlastingly tied,
>> ' CHRIS. HATTON.'

SCENE IV.—*A street in London.*

Enter BURLEIGH *and* JOHN MELVILLE, *in conversation.*

BURLEIGH.

Ah, John, it is a merry world indeed
To lookers-on.   'Tis full of humorous stuff
To cause them laughter; but to those who take
A part in this performance, and who help
To mix things up—although against their will—
It is a serious task.

MELVILLE.

I know it, Cecil; yea, I've learnt all this
To my discomfiture.   For what we're born
I'm oft in serious doubt.   I'm sure 'tis not
To make things smooth.   It is beyond our skill.
The earth itself is made of ups and downs,
And so, methinks, our lives must be.

BURLEIGH.

I would I could invent a way whereby
They could be levelled.

MELVILLE.

As long as we are ruled by sovereigns
Who know not their own minds, it were lost time
To ponder o'er it long.

BURLEIGH.

This villain Leicester will disturb us all,
I can foresee.   His insolence will know
No bounds, and when let loose it will befoul
The very air we breathe and poison us.
Whilst he's alive I dread what's like to happen.

MELVILLE.

Well, Cecil, to bewail our fate will not
Preserve us from it.   We will do our duty,
And thus enjoy the surer happiness
Of doing right.

BURLEIGH.

'Tis not my own fate I lament, but 'tis
The nation's.   Think of what's in store for it.

MELVILLE.

Leave it to do its duty, Burleigh.

BURLEIGH.

What is its duty to a queen who doth
Allow a vain, ambitious, vicious man

To counsel her?   Thou couldst not blame it,
    John,
If it did murmur loudly.

MELVILLE.

Ah, Cecil, 'tis a problem far beyond
My skill to solve.

BURLEIGH.

          I hope to God
She'll find it out ere long.

MELVILLE.

With all my heart I echo thee.
               [Exeunt both.

Enter SUSSEX *and* LORD LINCOLN.

SUSSEX.

          What dost thou fear?

LINCOLN.

              O God!
Is there not much to fear?

SUSSEX.

            Tut! tut!
The queen's too changeful nature gives us hope.
'Tis but a passing whim of hers.   She'll tire
Of him again ere long.   He hath not skill

7

To stand on dizzy heights.   His heart gets weak;
His mind grows faint ; his head doth whirl, and
    down
He falls.   He's skilful in the climbing up,
But he doth lose his balance on the top.
If needful, there's a way to bring him down
With greater certainty.

LINCOLN.

Pray how ?

SUSSEX.

To make the height to which he seeks to climb
More slippery.

LINCOLN.

I cannot reach thy meaning.

SUSSEX.

Why, make the queen suspicious ; tell her how
He boasts of conquering her ; of how she fears
To do what would displease him ; how he says,
And she doth quickly, gladly do ; yea, how
He scorns her in his heart.   This is a way
That will most surely bring him low—as low
As is the grave itself.

LINCOLN.

I'm glad on it.

I am more hopeful now.

SUSSEX.

Then we may tell her of the nation's tears
And murmurings, and prophesy a storm
From it that will, with mighty violence,
Disturb her throne.   Methinks such news as this
Would almost cure her of itself.

LINCOLN.

Pray God it will!
[*Exeunt both.*

Re-enter BURLEIGH, *with* LEICESTER.

BURLEIGH.

I'm glad that thou art reconciled to her.

LEICESTER.

I tell thee, Burleigh, she is in my power.
She loves me far more deeply than she did;
Nor would I wonder if she married me.

BURLEIGH.

Nay, nor would I.
Methinks she will.   I've noted with what deep
Regard she bends to thee.   I would that I
Were in thy place.

LEICESTER.

No doubt thou dost.
And there are many more who have the same

Deep wish; yea, many more who envy me
And hate me with undying hate.

BURLEIGH.

Nay!

LEICESTER.

I know them well. The queen doth know them,
too.

BURLEIGH.

It cannot be.
They cannot hate thee so.

LEICESTER.

Ha, ha!
How innocent thou art!

BURLEIGH.

Perchance thou knowest more than I?

LEICESTER.

Thou know'st a little, too.

BURLEIGH.

A little? yea, 'tis true.
Not near so much as thou dost seem to know.
How dost thou mean to punish them?

LEICESTER.

I will devise a little torture that
Will cure them well.

BURLEIGH.

               Nay,
Thou canst afford to be more merciful.
Pray, let me intercede for them.

LEICESTER.

           I'd counsel thee
To intercede for thine own self.

                   [Exeunt both.

SCENE V.—*France.   Garden at the Palace at Blois.*

Enter CATHERINE DE MEDICIS *and* CHARLES IX.
in conversation.

CATHERINE.

Thou art too faint of heart to be a king.
Thou art not bold enough to slay thy foes.
Come, pluck up courage, son, and show thyself
A man, and fit to rule the mighty France.

CHARLES.

It is not courage that I need, but 'tis
A cruel heart.

CATHERINE.

Ha, ha!
A cruel heart, indeed!   A cruel heart
To kill thy enemies!   It is not just
To make thyself secure? to serve thy God?
And to preserve His Church?   'Tis cruelty!
Thou'lt treat with kindness those who plot thy
     fall?
With gentleness the men who seek thy death?
Nay, thou wouldst aid thy foes to murder thee?
Would draw the dagger to thy breast?   Most
     strange!
I have a bold and grateful son indeed;
My country has a brave and resolute king;
The Church I love a noble champion.
I would I had not given thee birth.

CHARLES.

Nay, mother,
Thou dost not count the cost of what thou urgest.

CATHERINE.

The cost!
What can it cost?   I know the recompense—
Glory and peace, and great prosperity.
Who are these canting hypocrites? these foes
Of God and man? these stirrers-up of strife?
What is their mission here?   What is their use

In this most busy world ?   To plot and scheme ;
To be the enemies of peace ; to spread
Dismay and ruin ; yea, to threaten men
Of piety and holiness.   To curse,
To put to death such serpents, beasts, and worms,
Would be a holy act, and would obtain
The sanction of our justice-loving God.
I urge thee to this deed of justice, son,
Because I'd have thee be the instrument
To do God's will.   When thou and I are dead,
Posterity will bless us for this work.

CHARLES.

I see it is my duty, mother.

CATHERINE.

                    Thy duty ! yea.
Our duty is to seek and know God's will,
And to perform it, though it bring us hate.
To take deep vengeance on His enemies
Is what He seeks from us, and those who have
The power to do it are His chosen ones.
Thy brother comes this way, and wearing smiles.

Enter ALENÇON.

Well, son, what means this joyousness ?

ALENÇON.

I have received glad news from Fénelon.
Elizabeth is well disposed to me,
And speaks in hopeful terms of our betrothal.
Is that not cause for joyousness?

CATHERINE.

It is, my son.
It gives me wondrous cheer to hear this news.
What doth he say?

ALENÇON.

That she regards me as a noble prince,
A brave and valiant man; that she doth ask
For proofs of my affection every day,
And reads with no concealèd joy my letters.

CATHERINE.

'Tis well.
I can assure thee this is evidence
That love is growing in her heart. I know
Its mode of growth in woman far too well
To be deceived. Is there aught else he said?

ALENÇON.

That more than all she was impressed by what
She thought was written to De Foix. (*Laughs.*)

CATHERINE (*smiling*).

Ah! ah!
We will not laugh at such simplicity,
But mourn that thou must marry such a one,
To glorify thy country and thy Church.
Thou speedest well, my son.   I see this England,
This proud, imperious, yet most silly queen,
The slaves of France.   I see the Catholic Church
Implanted on the soil where heresy
Doth thrive.   I see beloved France rise up
And rule the world, and ye the arbiters
'Tween nations, men, and God Himself.   How
    blest
Am I, the mother of such sons!

[*Exeunt all.*

SCENE VI.—*Westminster.   A room in the Palace.*

Enter QUEEN ELIZABETH *and* FÉNELON *in conversation*

ELIZABETH.

Thou hast not been explicit with me, Fénelon.

FÉNELON.

Nay, madam, I have told thee all I know.

ELIZABETH.

But thou hast not.

FÉNELON.

What have I left unsaid?

ELIZABETH.

A wondrous deal.
Thou hast not said what compensation I
Shall have for the injury to his face.

FÉNELON.

Himself, good lady.
The hurt is disappearing rapidly,
And soon his face will be as clear as thine;
And as thine is the loveliest on earth,
Thou canst not find a fault with his.

ELIZABETH.

It cannot be.
Small-pox is never cured.

FÉNELON.

Pardon, madam,
But hast thou evidence of this?

ELIZABETH.

I have been told by skilful men.

FÉNELON.

Then, they have told thee lies.   It is not so.
In France it is a common cure, and there
Is one who hath attained great skill in this.
'Tis he attends on my good master.

ELIZABETH.

I would that thou couldst bring him over here.

FÉNELON.

I'll try, sweet lady.
Thou wilt be pleased with him.   Apart from this
He is a worthy man.

ELIZABETH.

Thy master, too, is short, and I am tall.

FÉNELON.

'Tis very well.
He cannot be thy master, then, for thou
Couldst rule him easily.

ELIZABETH.

'Tis said he hath a big and ugly mouth.

FÉNELON.

It is a lie.
'Tis true, his mouth is not so beautiful
As thine, for thine is perfect, yet it is
A mouth that would not sour thy kisses.

ELIZABETH.

His legs are crooked, too.

FÉNELON.

I know not, lady, who hath told thee this,
But he had crooked eyes.

ELIZABETH.

And, then, he hath a monstrous head.

FÉNELON.

But 'tis not empty, madam, thou'lt confess.

ELIZABETH.

I have my doubts of it.

FÉNELON.

What! after all he's written to thee? Thou hast
Confessed his thoughts and words are beautiful.
Doth beauty grow in barren ground?

ELIZABETH.

But words are easily writ.

FÉNELON.

                        True, madam.
But 'tis not given to every man to write
In language choice and beautiful. It is
A gift of bounteous Nature, and of which
She's sparing, too.

ELIZABETH.

I would that I had such a gift!

FÉNELON.

Thou canst not doubt thy own rare skill, sweet
    lady!
I can assure thee thou art envied greatly
By all who long to be admired for
Their grace of diction.

ELIZABETH.

    This is but flattery.

FÉNELON.

If truth is flattery, I grant it, lady.
If it is flattering the sun to say
He doth impart the greatest warmth and light,
We speak but truthfully, and so I speak
The truth in saying that thy eloquence
Is rare and wonderful, and doth entrance
The heart of him who hears thee speak and reads
The words thou writest.

ELIZABETH.

As I grow old—and I am old, God knows—
I feel the skill and beauty I possessed
When young are slipping rapidly away.

FÉNELON.

It is thy great humility, good lady.
Thou art as humble as thou'rt beautiful
And wise.   It is so in God's world.   'Tis they
On whom He hath bestowed the greatest gifts
Who are less conscious of their precious worth.
In every priceless gift thou shinest, yet
Thou art most humble.   Were it otherwise,
Thou wouldst not be so loved and worshipped.

ELIZABETH.

Yet it is nature's law that beauty fades
As age creeps on.

FÉNELON.

                    Most true ;
And that doth evidence that by divine
Protecting Providence thou art used kindly.
For thee the laws of nature are reversed :
The older thou dost get—for thou canst not
Expect to live thy youthful days again—
More beautiful thou seem'st to be ; so none
Can wonder why men love thee so.

[Exeunt both.

ACT IV.

SCENE I.—*Westminster. A room in the Palace.*

Enter QUEEN ELIZABETH, *alone.*

ELIZABETH.

                    Ah, marriage!
It is a joy that I shall never know.
The time for best enjoying it is past.
I wear a crown, indeed, but not the crown
Of happiness. I've let the years slip by
Of indecision and of playing with the love
I could have had, and now I taste the fruit—
Most bitter fruit—of what I sowed. They say
I am most wise. Ha! ha! If I'd been wise,
I would have seen old age creep on and gloom.
That is not wisdom that doth ever gaze
On passing beauty, and doth shut its eyes
To Nature's ugliness. They flatter me
To say I'm wise. I gaze upon my youth
As one doth gaze upon a fairy land

In dreams : it is receding from my view,
And in its place a dreary solitude
Doth rise, o'er which I have to travel.   Alas!
Sweet company could cheer me on.   I fear
To tread so dark a path alone.   O God!
I do repent me now of ill-spent youth.

Enter KATE ASHLEY.

Ah, Kate! thou lov'st me well?

KATE ASHLEY.

What means your majesty?   Thou canst not
    doubt
My love for thee?

ELIZABETH.

I would that all could love me as dost thou;
And yet I cannot hope for it.   Ah, Kate!
I may command, and they may not refuse
To do.   'Twere wise of them; but I have not
The power to command their love.   Alas!
I cannot read their hearts.   I would I could,
For I should read strange language there.

KATE ASHLEY.

Thou canst not make them love thee, it is true,
If they prefer to hate thee, yet thou dost
Possess the wondrous skill to read their hearts.

It is a gift which God hath given to thee,
Along with other gifts divine.

ELIZABETH.

Thou hast no evidence of this.

KATE ASHLEY.

Yea, overwhelming evidence, sweet lady.
I've seen and heard thee speak to many men,
Who did protest their mighty love for thee ;
And yet thou didst lay ope their very hearts,
And found it written there that they had love
For no one but themselves.   Then I have seen
How others would have urged thee to a deed
Of monstrous cruelty, because 'twould save
Thyself and throne—because 'twas just, indeed.
And then most skilfully thou madest them all
Confess they sought their own most selfish ends.
Yea, many instances I could sum up
To prove thy wondrous skill.

ELIZABETH.

   I little thought, sweet Kate,
I was observed with such intent by thee.
Come, tell me, dost thou think that I am loved ?

KATE ASHLEY.

   I cannot doubt it, madam.
Who could not love so kind and sweet a creature?

8

It were a heart of stone, unnatural,
That could not love thee. Yea, I warrant me,
Such hearts are rare in England now. It is
Confessed by all thou art a worthy queen,
And dost deserve to rule a mighty land.

ELIZABETH.
                    I thank thee, Kate,
For such sweet words. They're curing medicine
For aching grief.

KATE ASHLEY.
                    Why dost thou grieve?

ELIZABETH.

Because 'tis natural. Dost think that queens
Should never grieve?

KATE ASHLEY.
                              Alas!
I know that all are heirs to it. Methinks
Thou hast enough to make thee grieve.

ELIZABETH.
              Indeed, I have, my Kate.
I have a heavy weight to bear. Alas!
I often think my strength will not last out,
And that 'twill drag me down.

KATE ASHLEY.

      Nay, never fear.
Thou hast around thee willing, trusty aids,
To help thee bear thy burden.

ELIZABETH.

      Nay, Kate,
I have suspicion of them all. I'll trust
Myself. If I'm too feeble to support
My kingdom, they will never prop it up.
The legs would be unequal, Kate, and so
The kingdom would be bent in many shapes.
The longer props would kick the shorter down,
Until the whole would fall and ruin them.
I'd grieve for thee, sweet Kate, if I should die.

KATE ASHLEY.

But thou wilt live for many years.

ELIZABETH.

     Pray God I shall!
I would not like to die.

Enter LADY SHEFFIELD *and* FRANCES HOWARD.

What message bear ye, ladies? For I see
'Tis burdensome.

LADY SHEFFIELD.

It is, sweet lady, for it doth affect
The life of one good man, who loves thee well.

FRANCES HOWARD.

Yea, deeper than the loud-toned love of some.

ELIZABETH.

I love all those who truthfully love me.

LADY SHEFFIELD.

Pray be it so for this poor man, for I
Will swear his love is truth itself.

ELIZABETH.

Thou art no feeble advocate, indeed.
Come, tell me who it is.

LADY SHEFFIELD.

Thy noble vice-chamberlain, who's sick to death
Because thou wilt not smile on him.

FRANCES HOWARD.

He longs to have a gracious word from thee
Before he dies.

ELIZABETH.

                Poor lids !
And is he stricken so ?

FRANCES HOWARD.

          Yea, lady;
He cannot rise from off his bed.

ELIZABETH.

    And all for love of me?

FRANCES HOWARD.

For love of thee.

ELIZABETH.

          Poor sheep!
And doth he feel himself a wanderer,
And little cared for?

LADY SHEFFIELD.

         Yea, lady;
Far from the fold he loves, where he deserves
To be, far more than many there.

FRANCES HOWARD.

Where there are many wolves in sheep's disguise.

ELIZABETH.

         I'll write to him.
I know he loves me truly, though he is
A jealous-minded man. I'd grieve most deeply
If he should die for want of my sad smiles.

LADY SHEFFIELD.

Sad smiles, indeed ! Who says thy smiles are
sad ?

FRANCES HOWARD.

He hath an evil eye who told thee so.

ELIZABETH.

'Tis said my smiles are sad.

LADY SHEFFIELD.

It is not true, sweet lady, for thy smiles
Are sorrow-curers, bringers of deep joy.

FRANCES HOWARD.

They lighten dreary lives.

ELIZABETH.

Pray, tell him I forgive him all his rashness,
And ask him come again.

BOTH.

We thank thee, gracious majesty.

[*Exeunt ladies.*

ELIZABETH.

There's one who loves me, Kate, to whom I've
done
A cruel wrong.

KATE ASHLEY.

Nay, thou hast not.
He doth deserve it all.

ELIZABETH.

Nay, dost thou think so ?

KATE ASHLEY.

He did presume too much upon thy love.
Nay, even if ye looked at other men
He censured thee.   That was not gratitude.
He's reaping now what he hath sown, and thou
Hast acted wisely.

ELIZABETH.

And dost thou think I've punished him enough ?

KATE ASHLEY.

'Twould do no harm
To have him near thee once again.

ELIZABETH.

I'll have him, Kate,
For I do sorrow for him much.

KATE ASHLEY.

Thou hast a gentle heart.

ELIZABETH.

I would I had a gentler, Kate.

Enter LA MOTTE FÉNELON.

But who comes here ?   Pray leave me for awhile.

KATE ASHLEY (*aside*).
    I hate this sly ambassador.
He hath no goodly mission here. [*Exit* KATE.

FÉNELON.
Good-morrow, gentle lady.

ELIZABETH.
    Good-morrow, Fénelon.
I hope thou hast good news.

FÉNELON.
    Nay, I have not, sweet lady.
I bring depressing news.

ELIZABETH.
     Well, out with it.

FÉNELON.
My master is aweary of delay.

ELIZABETH.
     Ah, sir,
He's too impatient : he must curb his love.

FÉNELON.

        Must curb his love ?
What dost thou ask ? Can love be curbed ? I thought
It was no bridled horse.

ELIZABETH.

      Then learn from me
It can be curbed. Necessity is that
Which Nature's laws may teach.

FÉNELON.

If love is curbed with ease, I doubt its truth.
'Tis very weak, at least.

ELIZABETH.

     True love is proved
By how it lasts, and how it fights against
The stress of circumstance. The longer it
Doth love, the greater strength it has.
How is thy master ?

FÉNELON.

    Quite love-sick, madam.

ELIZABETH.

Such sickness can be easily cured.

FÉNELON.

Nay, madam ;
He hath a serious attack, indeed,
Beyond the skill of man to cure.   It is
A sickness unto death.   'Tis thou alone
Who hath the power to rouse him up.

ELIZABETH.

What power have I ?
Am I the only queen in this great world ?

FÉNELON.

Nay, canst thou ask ?
Thou art the only queen whom he could love.
Thou art the only queen who doth deserve
Such love as he can give.   Thou art so wise,
So beautiful, so virtuous, so gentle,
That loving thee is wondrous natural.
It seems beyond our power to treat thee other
Than worshipping and loving thee.   If thus
Thy nature doth attract the love of all,
Pray think how it would quickly, strongly grow
In my poor master's heart.

ELIZABETH.

Ah, Fénelon,
Thou art no feeble advocate of thy
Poor master.   Pray, tell him this from me, that I

Feel sure of his deep love for me ; that I
Am grateful for such honest, noble love ;
And that it shall not live without reward.

FÉNELON.

I thank thee, lady.
Thy message will revive him much, but not
To perfect joy. I would that thou couldst give
Much surer hope.

ELIZABETH.

I cannot.
Be satisfied with what I've said.

FÉNELON.

I will, fair lady.
[*Exit* FÉNELON.

ELIZABETH.

Methinks that love is growing in my heart
For this wise prince. Nay, I am sure of it.
I long to marry him, but that I fear
The nation will not sanction it. 'Twould rise
In anger 'gainst a prince who hates the Church
My subjects love. That is the obstacle
I know not how to overcome. My council
Would fan the flame into a fearful blaze
I dread would scorch my throne. The only way
To gain my ends would be to bribe them all

With promises of favour and reward.
Refusal shall but hurl them to disgrace,
Which they will dread more than my marriage
    with
The prince they hate.   I'll let no time slip by
Ere I commence the task.   [*Exit.*

SCENE II.—*A street in London.   Enter* TWO
    GENTLEMEN *in conversation.*

1ST GENT.

I've heard but little of the news; if thou dost
know much more, I beg thou wouldst enlighten
me.

2ND GENT.

Thou know'st that something terrible hath
stirred the minds of all, and that the faces thou
dost see bespeak some poignant grief?

1ST GENT.

I've never seen the citizens so sorrowful in my
time, friend.

2ND GENT.

Nor hast thou ever heard of such a fiendish
crime.   Pray God it is the worst and last!

1ST GENT.

I'll share thy wish if thou wilt give me cause
for it.

2ND GENT.

I'll give thee most abundant cause for it. The
infidel and devilish King and Queen of France
did butcher, on St. Bartholomew's day, all the
Protestants in their homes. 'Twas done by
serpent stealth, when they were helpless and
unable to defend themselves. O God! how
canst thou let such fiends live?

1ST GENT.

Thou needst might ask, my friend. His ways
are wondrous strange.

2ND GENT.

No doubt He'll punish them in time.

1ST GENT.

I hope He'll burn them with hell-fire. [*Exeunt.*

Enter SUSSEX *and* BURLEIGH.

BURLEIGH.

No deed could better serve our ends or damn
Their own. They are their own worst enemies.
The queen will never countenance so great
And deep a crime; the nation's hate will be

Increased, and less and less they'll be inclined
To favour marriage with this ugly prince.
The storm I see is rising now will soon
Become a whirlwind which she dare not face.
For my own part, I'm glad on it.

SUSSEX.

And I am deeply sorrowful.

BURLEIGH.

And why, my lord?

SUSSEX.

So many murdered innocents is cause
For grief.

BURLEIGH.

But it will save our country and our queen.

SUSSEX.

Salvation based upon a hideous crime
Is an unnatural fruit, and shares the fate
Of all misgendered things—a useless life
And speedy death.

BURLEIGH.

Thou'rt in thy quiet, thinking mood to-day.
To-morrow thou'lt think different.

SUSSEX.

I'd rather let them wed than have a crime
So terrible an obstacle.

BURLEIGH.

That he may murder us!   Nay, Sussex, nay.
Thou art not serious?

SUSSEX.
I am, indeed,

Most serious.

BURLEIGH.
It is a serious dream.

SUSSEX.

We'll see; we'll see.

[*Exeunt.*

SCENE III.—*A room in* SIR CHRISTOPHER
HATTON'S *house.*

Enter SIR CHRISTOPHER HATTON *and* WHITLEY.

HATTON.

Ah, I'm a happy man to-day, good Whitley.

WHITLEY.

I'm glad thou'rt in a joyous mood, but I've
Grave doubts how long 'twill last.

HATTON.

        Until I die, good man.
The clouds of her ill-will have passed away,
And now the glorious sun doth shine.

WHITLEY.

But other clouds may come.

HATTON.

        Nay, Whitley.
I see none coming on.   Yea, what I see
Is one expanse of brilliant sky.

WHITLEY.

And this in spite of her too changeful mood?

HATTON.

        Yea, in spite of that.
Methinks her moods are not so changeable.
They may appear so, but when thou dost think
Of all the varied natures she must please,
She needs must show a varied nature, too.
We think she's changeable because she has
So many rare and wondrous gifts.

WHITLEY.

But didst thou think so when she cast thee off?

HATTON.

I own, good Whitley, I was wrong. I own
That I deserved such punishment. I am
A jealous-minded man, and when I see
She favours others whom I think would do
Her wrong, my anger urges me to speak
My mind. I have no mastery o'er myself,
And when too late I grieve. Indeed, I see
She hath been merciful to me. If others
Had done what I have done; had shown the
 spleen
That I have shown; had uttered words that I
Have said, they'd be bemoaning in the Tower;
Whereas the greatest punishment that she
Hath meted out to me is banishment
From her sweet face, although I cannot bear
E'en that. But I'm to gaze on it again.
And with what joy I'll kiss her hand once more!
How zealous I shall be to please her well!
How sharp a curb I'll keep on jealousy
And anger! How guarded shall my language
 be!
I would not suffer o'er again the days
Of sorrow and of gloom which now are o'er!
    [*Exeunt* HATTON *and* WHITLEY.

9

SCENE IV.—*A room in the house of the* COUNTESS
OF ESSEX.

Enter the COUNTESS OF ESSEX, *alone.*

I sometimes feel he'll never marry me,
In spite of that great love he doth protest.
He'd risk too much. The queen would banish
    him
Beyond forgiveness ; yea, would hate us both,
And thrust us in the Tower to drag our lives
Apart. She is a selfish, cruel queen,
Ungrateful, undeserving faithful love,
For she would never let us know its joy.
How many young and hopeful lives hath she
Destroyed, because they married 'gainst her wish !
Should we escape her rage and spleen ? Nay,
    nay !
But yet my love would risk it all.

Enter LEICESTER.

    My queen ! (*Kisses her.*)

COUNTESS OF ESSEX.

Am I thy queen indeed ? Nay, hast thou not
Mistaken me ?

LEICESTER.

Ah, jealous still ? Thou hast no need to be ;
I have not given thee cause.

COUNTESS OF ESSEX.

Forgive me, Dudley.   Thou canst understand.
I hear so much of how she favours thee
That I must needs be envious.

LEICESTER.

She'd be more envious if she could read
My heart.

COUNTESS OF ESSEX.

What would she read there, Dudley ?

LEICESTER.

Dost thou not know ?   'Tis not concealed from
    thee.

COUNTESS OF ESSEX.

Nay, I am blind.   Pray, read it me.

LEICESTER.

That I love none but thee.   That thou alone
Wilt be my wife.

COUNTESS OF ESSEX.

Why do they say thou'lt marry the queen ?

LEICESTER.

Who say so lie.   I'll never marry her.
She doth already know the one she'll wed.

COUNTESS OF ESSEX.

Pray, whom?

LEICESTER.

The Duc d'Alençon.

COUNTESS OF ESSEX.

Nay?

LEICESTER.

She is resolved to marry him.

COUNTESS OF ESSEX.

I thought she hated ugly men.

LEICESTER.

She doth, but somehow she believes he's not
So ugly as reports would make him be.
Indeed, she says he is a handsome man,
A wise and noble prince, and worthy her.
La Motte hath filled her mind with all these lies,
And she hath great regard for him.   Who tries
To tell her truth doth run great risk, for she
Doth silence him with threats.

COUNTESS OF ESSEX.

The country will be sorely grieved at this,
For it will be in bondage to the Pope.

LEICESTER.

My policy will be
To urge this marriage on. 'Twill please the
    queen,
And court the favour of our future king.
I'm now resolved to marry thee at once,
If thou'lt consent.

COUNTESS OF ESSEX.

With all my heart.
But wilt thou let her know?

LEICESTER.

Nay, nay!
We'll wed in secrecy, unknown to her.
If she had knowledge of it, sweet, the joys
Of married life would be but short.

COUNTESS OF ESSEX.

Alas! they would.

SCENE V.—*An apartment in the Palace.*

Enter ELIZABETH *and* FÉNELON.

ELIZABETH.

I'm grieved at heart.
Wouldst thou extenuate so base a deed?
Thou art as bad as they.

FÉNELON.

Indeed, sweet lady,
Thou canst not be so grieved as I, or they.
My king and queen hath done this evil deed,
And now are suffering torments terrible ;
Yea, such a grief I fear will drive them mad.
I pray thee, let this have full weight with thee
In judging them.   It was excess of zeal,
Of love of God, that urged them to remove
Whom they regarded as His bitterest foes.

ELIZABETH.

Nay, nay !
They know that God doth never countenance
The wholesale slaughter of His children whom
He loves.   Another motive urged them on.
Dost think they would invite the hate and scorn,
The horror of the world through love of God ?
Alas ! our love for Him is not so deep.
True love for God gives birth to deeds of peace.
I know thy mistress and thy master well,
And know they're both ambitious.

FÉNELON.

And what is their ambition, my good lady ?
'Tis to promote the welfare of the Church

They love ; to make the country which they rule,
The people whom they govern, great and vast.
Is that a natural desire for kings
And queens ?   Is it a selfish one ?   Dost thou
Not wish to serve thy country well ?   Indeed,
Wouldst thou be fit to govern if thou hadst
No hope and wish of such a noble kind ?
No man could call thee selfish, nay, could not
Describe thee scornfully as most ambitious.
Then I would ask thee, lady, not to judge
My mistress too untenderly.

ELIZABETH.

I judge them far more tenderly than they
Have judged the victims of their rage.   Dost
    think
The greatness of a nation is secure
When built upon a hideous crime ?   Nay, that
Prosperity will grow on fetid soil ?
Can drinking human blood impart deep joy ?
Yea, Fénelon, those are the truest kings
And queens who would promote the nation's
    good ;
But they are truer far when they promote
And base it on good deeds.   Thy mistress sets
Her kingdom up on soil in which 'twill sink
Much lower down than e'er it was before.

FÉNELON.

　　　　　　　　I do confess
They have been blind and acted foolishly,
But which of us hath never erred, and who
Hath never known what blindness is?　There comes
A time in each man's life when he is blind,
And moves in darkness, stumbling on his way
To find the light.　Some chance on it by luck,
But others see a glimmer in the gloom
For which they steer; but e'er they reach it down
They fall, in deeper darkness still.　So hath
My mistress been deceived, and so is she
Now struggling in the gloom and with the fears
That it doth breed.　'Twere nobler if we lent
A tender help to bring her forth from there,
Than force her further down.　Methinks that God
Doth make us blind at times, that we may give
An opportunity for every man
To guide us right, and he who guides us wrong,
Or without pity lets us go astray,
Doth sin most grievously.

ELIZABETH.

　　　　　　　　'Tis truly spoken.
I'll think it o'er, yea, I will think it o'er.

I would ye left me now, that I may spend
My time in thought.

FÉNELON.

I will, sweet lady.
Thy nature is so kind and merciful,
That I feel sure thou wilt with tenderness
Regard this hasty deed.

[*Exit* FÉNELON.

ELIZABETH.

Ah, Fénelon,
Thou think'st that thou hast conquered me.   'Tis
    well !
But thou wilt be deceived e'er long, poor man !
To thy discomfiture.   I'll use thee first,
Because I find in thee a useful tool ;
But when thou'rt done with I can cast thee off.
'Tis thou art blind, though thou dost think,
    with no
Slight scorn of me, that it is I.   I'll ope
Thy eyes in time, but in a way thou'lt least
Expect.   I will not quarrel with thy king
And queen !   Nay, nay !   I know a wiser move.
Blind !   He who shuts his eyes, then stabs his foe,
Is blind ?   Dost think I am a child ?   God's
    death !
I'll child thee, upstart ! thou wilt find, too late,

Thou hast a queen to deal with, who can shut
Her eyes to strike a blow at him she hates.

Enter BURLEIGH.

Ha! my lord Cecil.

BURLEIGH.

Thou didst send for me, good lady?

ELIZABETH.

   Come, sit thee down,
And let us seriously talk. What dost thou think
Of this vile murder done in France?

BURLEIGH.

What dost thou think of it?

ELIZABETH.

   I wish to know thy thoughts,
Not tell thee mine.

BURLEIGH.

   Indeed, fair madam,
I know not what to think of it.

ELIZABETH.

   Thou dost not know?
Come, speak thy mind, for thou dost surely know
How thou dost look on it.

BURLEIGH.

Yea,
I know how I do look on it, but what
To think on it I do not know.

ELIZABETH.

How dost thou look on it?

BURLEIGH.

With horror, lady.

ELIZABETH.

Most natural, indeed.
And so thy thoughts must be allied?

BURLEIGH.

I am divided in my thoughts.

ELIZABETH.

Pray, what divides them, man?

BURLEIGH.

The weakness of mankind.

ELIZABETH.

Nay, is thy brain so weak?

BURLEIGH.

Nay, madam,
It is no jesting time.

ELIZABETH.

      Then tell me, Cecil,
Have they not done a most unpardonable crime,
And thus deserved our hate?

BURLEIGH.

      Methinks they have;
A crime I'll never pardon.

ELIZABETH.

       Nay, say not so.

BURLEIGH.

I'd say it with my dying breath.

ELIZABETH.

      Thou couldst not, Cecil.

BURLEIGH.

And why, I pray?

ELIZABETH.

Because thou hast a most forgiving heart.

BURLEIGH.

      I have, indeed,
But not for such a crime.

ELIZABETH.

For such a crime, I say.

BURLEIGH.

Methinks I never could.

ELIZABETH.

          Ha!

Thou dost not know of what thou'rt capable :
But I know well.

BURLEIGH.

Thou hast more knowledge of my heart than I.

ELIZABETH.

          I have, indeed.

But I would speak to thee more seriously,
Yet in a place more secret than this room ;
So come with me.

      [*Exeunt* ELIZABETH *and* BURLEIGH.

Enter LADY SHEFFIELD *and* FRANCES HOWARD.

FRANCES HOWARD.

Yea, if I knew it I would tell her straight.
I'd drag him down.

LADY SHEFFIELD.

And yet, methinks, he'd never risk it.

FRANCES HOWARD.

          Methinks he would.

If I were told to-morrow he had married
The countess, it would not surprise me.

LADY SHEFFIELD.

Nay!

FRANCES HOWARD.

The Earl of Leicester, as we know, is sly
And crafty, but there is a way to snare
The fox.   But here comes Kate.

Enter KATE ASHLEY.

Good-morrow, Kate!

KATE ASHLEY.

Good-morrow, ladies; what's abroad?

FRANCES HOWARD.

The Earl of Leicester's married.

KATE ASHLEY.

Nay!

FRANCES HOWARD.

'Tis true.

LADY SHEFFIELD.

Nay, Kate;
'Tis but a rumour we have heard.

FRANCES HOWARD.

But rumours are most often true.

KATE ASHLEY.

           Yea, yea.
But he would never dare to marry.

FRANCES HOWARD.

What dost thou know he'd dare?

KATE ASHLEY.

I know he'd never dare to vex the queen,
As he hath done before.

FRANCES HOWARD.

How could he vex her if she knew it not?

KATE ASHLEY.

                  True.
But if it reaches thee, the world will know,
And thus her majesty will hear of it.

FRANCES HOWARD.

          I hope she will, indeed.
She'll make his joy short-lived.

KATE ASHLEY.

               Ah!
I have no sympathy for him.   He is
A man who forfeits love.

LADY SHEFFIELD.

He is an overweening wretch, a cur,
A puppet ; nor care I who kicks him down.

FRANCES HOWARD.

He will be kicked, ere long,
And most ungently, too.

[*Exeunt the three ladies.*

Re-enter ELIZABETH *and* BURLEIGH.

ELIZABETH.

What matter what my subjects think ?   Should
    they
Dictate to thee or me our every act ?
What use are kings and queens, indeed, if they
Must only do what meets their subjects' wish ?
What can the rabble know or see ?   What can
They reason out ?   Nay, could they tell thee what
They fear, if I should wed the duke ?   They cry
Aloud like children in the dark, because
They see a seeming shadow there.   I say,
They have been taught and urged to make this
    noise
By those whom I've marked out.   Nay, I will
    wed,
If only to revenge myself on them.
I know thou hast no cowardly fear.   I know

Why thou dost dread my marriage with the
    prince—
Because thou think'st he is not worthy me.
Nay, Cecil, rid thyself of such a fear.
He is a noble, pious prince and can
Become a goodly king. So rest secure,
And in the council aid my cause. I will
Reward thee as thou wilt deserve.

BURLEIGH.

                I fear, sweet lady,
My task will be a sorry one in face
Of such great odds.

ELIZABETH.

                The better for thee.
Thou'lt have me on thy side ; what matter then
Who cries thee down ? I will reward thee first,
And make them envious.

BURLEIGH.

                Nay, nay.
They'd scorn me more, indeed.

ELIZABETH.

                Well, I will do
As thou dost wish. So thou hast promised me
To help my marriage on. I'll not forget,
And will expect to see thee bravely fight.

                [*Exit* ELIZABETH.

10

BURLEIGH.

Yea, I am in a sorry plight, indeed.
I dread this marriage, and I hate this prince,
And yet I'm pledged to favour both.   O God!
I would I were a simple subject, not
A minister besieged and tossed about
By woman's whims!   I daily fall in snares
Which she doth cover o'er and make attractive.
I would that I were far away from here,
And treading on much surer ground.   Alas!
I've ventured in this treacherous land, and must
Abide it yet awhile.   I'll earn the scorn
Of all the world.   But yet what can I do?
No man could envy me.   I am a poor
And martyred wretch.

[Exit BURLEIGH.

SCENE VI.—*France.   A garden at the Castle of Blois.*

Enter CATHERINE *and* CHARLES IX.

CATHERINE.

          What dost thou fear?
Thou hast a craven heart.

CHARLES.

Our crime hath met the horror of the world.
All Christendom doth look on us with dread
And fright, and those who loved us once and our
Dear country hate us with undying hate.

CATHERINE.

    Then let them hate.
Our Pope and God doth love us still.

CHARLES.

    Ah, mother,
Thou art an enigma to me.

CATHERINE.

     To thee, no doubt,
Because thou hast not intellect enough
To reason out the simplest things.

CHARLES.

This murder is no simple thing——

CATHERINE.

     Murder
Pray, call it what it is—a pious act.

CHARLES.

I'll call it, then, a pious act. I well
Can see this pious act will drag us down.

We shall be looked upon by all the world
As though we're scorpions.

CATHERINE.

Nay.

I know the world, my son.   I know it well.
I knew it would be horrified, but yet
Not deeply so.   It will ere long forget
What we have done.   Its selfishness will cure
What it doth suffer now ; and when it sees
That hatred will not bring prosperity,
Nor will preserve it from its enemies,
It will return to love.   Now, son, what is
The worth of all its love or hate ?   Is it
As true as is the Pope's, as strong and deep
As God's ?   Is it not hate and selfishness
Disguised ?   'Tis cowardice, my son, that would
Commit as great a crime if it but had
The courage.   Here comes thy brother ; he, as I,
Doth glory in this deed.

Enter ALENÇON.

Nay, dost thou not ?

ALENÇON.

What dost thou ask ?

CATHERINE.

Thou dost regard it as a glorious deed
To rid our country of these heretics?

ALENÇON.

It is a deed o'er which we may rejoice
With most unbounded joy.   Why dost thou ask,
And doubt my ecstasy?

CATHERINE.

'Tis but to rouse thy brother up, for he
Doth suffer from some nervous fear.

ALENÇON.

Come, brother,
Why wear such gloomy looks?   Thou shouldst
be glad
And full of happiness, for thou art rid
Of thy most bitter foes.

CHARLES.

To make more bitter enemies.

CATHERINE.

He's past all cure.
I'll physic him no more.   No medicine
Will make the coward brave.

ALENÇON.

                                    Nay ;
Nor will the deed I contemplate remove
His gloominess.

CATHERINE.

                    What is it, son ?

ALENÇON.

When I am King of England I'll remove
By fire and sword those other heretics,
Who else will shake my throne, and make my life
Too insecure for peace of mind.   'Twill be
Another means to serve the Pope and God,
And set my country on a firmer base.
What matter though they hate us now, and wish
To ruin us ?   Their hate shall be short-lived.
Their foolish, love-sick queen shall be the means
Which shall destroy them utterly.

CATHERINE.

                              Bravo, my son !
I would thy brother were as brave as thou,
And were as true a king, as bold and fearless
A champion of his Church.   Yea, thou shalt be
Thy country's true deliverer, whom France
Shall honour as a God.   My noble son !

My pious, Christian son ! Yea, I rejoice
I gave thee birth, for thou hast blest my womb
Which bare thee, which thy brother else had
    cursed.
I would ye left me here awhile. I love
The solitude in which my thoughts alone
Are my most sweet companions.

ALENÇON.

       I know it, mother.
I'll go and leave thee to thyself awhile.
       [*Exeunt* CHARLES *and* ALENÇON.

CATHERINE.

Ah, life is strange and wondrous curious !
It lures us on by holding up far-off
Rewards whose glory dazzles us. Alas !
How eager are we all to get them in
Our grasp ! Our eyes are fixed on these alone,
Nor scarcely see the obstacles which strew
The path that leads to them. The paths which
    some
Must tread present far greater obstacles
Than hinder others, and demand more strength
And will to overcome them with success.
Such is my path, and I've displayed, indeed,
No common firmness in surmounting what

Would hinder me, yet where is my reward?
Where is that dazzling, brilliant prize I saw
When I set out? As when the sun doth shine
And make most objects glisten in its light
At distance off, but when we come quite close
The brilliance disappears, so hath the prize
Which drew me on quite vanished from my view.
I thought when I had rid belovèd France
Of these damned Protestants I should be free,
And know true peace of mind. Alas! the world
Seems duller, darker still, nor do I know
The peace which once I did enjoy. O Life!
Thy hopes are mere delusions, yea, methinks,
The false and treacherous beauty which allures
The traveller on, which decks and makes attrac-
   tive
The pitfalls into which he falls at last.

                                   [*Exit.*

SCENE VII.—*A street in London. Enter* SUSSEX
   and HATTON, *in conversation.*

SUSSEX.

         Nay, I am not surprised.
Our nature's made of such elastic stuff
That those who will may stretch it out to lengths
As suit their purpose best.

HATTON.

                           Our nature?
Why dost thou thus include thyself and me?

SUSSEX.

Yea, even thou and I are very weak,
And if we were in Burleigh's place, no doubt,
Would do as he.

HATTON.

But thou and I both sacrifice a deal
To act in opposition to the queen ;
And yet we have refused our aid to bring
This hateful marriage off.

SUSSEX.

I cannot judge him harshly, Chris, for he
Hath great excuse. Poor man! I know how
     Bess
Would wheedle him and touch his gentle heart
With strong entreaty and with honeyed words.
She knows where he is weak, and where he's
     strong
More deeply than thyself or I.   She is
A skilful player on the human heart,
And Burleigh's is an easy instrument.

HATTON.

She cannot play on thine and mine with such
Great skill, and so successfully.

SUSSEX.

      Be not so sure, my friend.
I've seen the time when thou thyself hast piped
Music both sweet and harsh as she hath bid ;
And I confess I've yielded to her skill
As uncontrollably.   Maybe, at last,
We'll urge this marriage on.

HATTON.

      Never, Sussex !
I'd rather see her buried than the spouse
Of such an ugly and deformed a wretch.
Oh, God ! that she should come to wed the son
Of such a monstrous mother !   Think of it,
My lord, and say if Heaven could look on it
With fav'ring eyes !

SUSSEX.

      It could not, Chris ;
But yet how many things are done on earth
Which please our God ?   I dread this marriage—
    yea,
No man could dread it more—and yet I am
So weak that I may lend my aid at last.

HATTON.

I'm sure thou never wilt.

SUSSEX.

I know my weakness best.

[*Exeunt.*

ACT V.

ELIZABETH.

Ah, Kate,
Love plays with us strange pranks. We think
we've fixed
Our love on one, and placed him on a height
Which others could not reach, when, as we gaze,
And seem content and sure of our great love,
The latter cools we know not how ; we know
Not when, indeed, till suddenly it seems
Most icy cold. We turn from him we loved
With discontent and scorn, almost with hate.
It is a law of nature, my sweet Kate,
Which greatly puzzles me.

KATE ASHLEY (*aside*).

Praise God!
It is confined to thee alone, else love
Would breed but universal grief.

ELIZABETH.

Methought I loved the prince with deeper love,
But now I could not marry him if he
Were perfect. Tell me, Kate, what says the
   world
Of my resolve to have no more of him?

KATE ASHLEY.

It doth rejoice
Most merrily.

ELIZABETH.

And is it pleased
With what I've done?

KATE ASHLEY.

In every town and village everyone
Doth weep for joy and laud thee to the skies.

ELIZABETH.

I'm glad on it.
Methinks that even I could weep for joy.
What cause do they assign for it?

KATE ASHLEY.

They think that thou hast sacrificed thyself
For love of them and of thy country. Thus,
They almost worship thee.

ELIZABETH.

         'Tis well, my Kate.
'Tis well they cannot guess the truer cause.

KATE ASHLEY (*aside*).

         'Tis well, indeed,
And yet 'twere better if it knew thou hadst
A mood less changeable.

ELIZABETH.

         Go, Kate;
Prepare my room and books for me. Methinks
I'll read awhile.   [*Exit* KATE ASHLEY.
         Yea, it is well.
I'm glad, indeed, to hear that ye rejoice.
I grudge it not, although it is not love
For ye that gives ye cause. This mirth would
    cease
If ye could know my love for Leicester is
As strong as e'er it was; that I'm resolved
To marry him—yea, marry him, in spite
Of all your tears and fears and threats. Are ye

Alone to have this happiness ?   Must I
Grow old and die, and never know the love
Of husband and of child ?   Nay, must I love,
But, unlike ye, be forced to stifle it ?
Is it the penalty of being a queen
That I must bear no fruit to beautify
And cheer fast-growing age ?   It cannot be ;
I have not strength or will to make it be.

[*Exit* ELIZABETH.

Enter LEICESTER.

A sorry plight !

I'm in no sorry plight.   'Tis true I'm wed,
And that's an obstacle which some would count
Quite insurmountable, but not to me.
I'll let no obstacle stand in my way
To be the king.   I'd risk my life for that.
'Tis true I've been o'er-hasty, yet who thought
The queen was not in earnest ?   She did seem
Most deep in love—so deep, indeed, that I
Could never hope to bring her out again.
I'll warrant me that none can read her heart.
She acts her part so well that none can tell
If it is jest or no.   Her love for me
Is what she never acts.   It is too real,
Too strong, and hath defied too many storms,
To be unsafe to trust.   She would have wed
Ere now but for this mighty obstacle,

Which she can never hope to overcome.
Though I repent I did not wait to see
The certain issue of this later love,
Yet I can feel at perfect liberty
To wed the queen.

(*He makes to go out, but the queen enters and*)
sees him.)

ELIZABETH.

                              Nay, stay.
I long to speak with thee.

LEICESTER (*turning round*).

                    Good-morrow, my good lady.

ELIZABETH.

How looks the world outside?

LEICESTER.

                    Most cheerful, madam.

ELIZABETH.

Nay, very bright and full of hope?

LEICESTER.

I see no speck of cloud to threaten storms.

ELIZABETH.

                    But clouds must come ere long.

LEICESTER.

'Twould be quite natural.

ELIZABETH.

Most threat'ning ones will come from France.

LEICESTER.

They'll never burst.

ELIZABETH.

Dost think they'll pass by harmlessly?

LEICESTER.

They cannot do us injury.

ELIZABETH.

Why cannot they?

LEICESTER.

Thy subjects' love would safely shelter thee
If they should burst.

ELIZABETH.

But love is not all-powerful.

LEICESTER.

It is the powerfullest thing on earth.

ELIZABETH.

Thou hast no proof of it.

11

LEICESTER.

I have the proof of my undying love.
No storm, however fiercely it did rage,
Could crush my love for thee.   Nay, think what
    storms
It hath withstood, and have they injured it ?
Methinks 'tis stronger now than e'er it was.

ELIZABETH.

I know thou hadst deep love for me, my lord,
When I was young ; but now I'm growing old
Thy love must be less strong.

LEICESTER.

Yea, on my knees, I'll swear it is as true,
As strong, as when I knew thee first.   Am I
Not growing old as thou, and can I hope
Once more to enjoy the love of youth ?
No maiden in her blushing teens could have
Attractions for me now.   Why dost thou doubt,
After it has been tried these many years,
My love for thee is dying out ?

ELIZABETH.

Because love feeds on beauty, and as I
Have lost the beauty of my youth, so will
Thy love have naught to nurture it.

LEICESTER.

Love doth not feed on outward loveliness.
'Tis true that fades, but inward beauty lives,
And in old age doth reach its perfect state.
Love feeds on virtue, truth, and piety,
All which thou'rt perfect in.   Where these are
     not
True love can not exist.   Nor hast thou lost,
Indeed, the beauty of thy outward form.
It doth improve as age creeps on.   My love
Need, therefore, never wither for the lack
Of blessed food.

ELIZABETH.

We will be seen and heard if we stay here.
Come, let us seek a more retired place,
And speak our thoughts, nor fear intrusion.

LEICESTER.

With all my heart, sweet madam.
          [*Exeunt* ELIZABETH *and* LEICESTER.

Enter LA MOTTE FÉNELON *and* LORD SUSSEX.

FÉNELON.

No simple girl at school would act as she.
They know their minds, at least, and what they
     like

And what they scorn, but your proud queen—
    alas!
I wonder that ye live, and that she hath
The constancy to sit upon a throne.

Sussex.

                    Ah, Fénelon,
I understand the disappointment that
Ye suffer from, and sympathize with ye.
No doubt it is a bitter grief to all
In France that they have failed in their bold
    schemes.
As doth the gambler feel, when he hath placed
At stake his own last coin, and loses it,
So must their sorrow be.   Methinks they played
A far too hazardous game to hope to win.
Hate cannot clothe herself in Love's bright robes
And look quite natural.   She must forget
At times she plays a part, and then she doth
Reveal unconsciously her decked-out self.

Fénelon.

Whate'er my master did, he showed he had
A purpose in his heart, a constant mind,
A firm, determined will—all qualities
As rare and admirable as virtue's self.
Thy mistress hath not found him out.   Her eyes
Are far too dull to notice his disguise.

Indeed, she doth believe he loves her yet,
But she hath cast him off because she loves
A life of coquetry.   She's very like
The butterfly that flies from flower to flower,
In great unrest.   This is no quality
To rule a country great as England is.
Methinks 'twill ruin it.

SUSSEX.

Ye need not fear, my lord.
She hath no love for human blood.   Methinks
I'd rather be the subject of a queen
Who had too soft a heart to put to death
Her rival and her fiercest enemy,
Than one who in cold blood, nor with remorse,
Could murder innocents and loving subjects,
Because they loved the Bible and their God,
And longed to know the truth.

FÉNELON.

My lord is ignorant of whom he speaks.
He doth not know their love of God and truth
Did make them plot against the throne.   My
        mistress
Removed in them most dangerous heretics,
Who sought to ruin France and kill their king
And queen.   I knew not truth was best displayed
By trait'rous acts.   I thank my noble lord

For teaching me.   He thus hath shown to me
That falsehood is more beautiful than truth.

SUSSEX.

Ha! ha!

Is that the reason why thou tellest lies?
And yet these falsehoods do not beautify
Thy countenance.   If I had taught thee this,
Thou wouldst not so contort thy face, but look
More loving, calm, and pleasant.   Ah! my lord
Doth think he can deceive me as he did
The queen.

FÉNELON (*aside*).

Curses on thee!

My God, I'll find a way to trip thee up.
I'll make thy face less beautiful, or else
I'll scorn myself.

Exeunt both.

Enter SIR CHRISTOPHER HATTON.

By Jupiter!   I'll round on her.   I'll speak
My thoughts; give utterance to the contempt
I feel for her.   I'll tell her with bold tongue
That she's not fit to be a queen.   To dangle,
And lovingly caress before us all,
This upstart Leicester is beyond my stock
Of patience to behold composedly

And keep a silent tongue.   I'll ope my mouth,
By God ! and fiery words shall scorch her up.
I would that I could burn him, too.   I'll wait
Until the devil has the task.

[Exit HATTON.

SCENE II.—-*Night.   A country place.*

Enter LEICESTER (disguised).

Ah, Leicester, thou art not so bold a man
As thou dost boast thyself to be, or else
Why dost thou tremble so ?   What makes thee
    start
At every little sound ? what makes thee fear
This talking solitude ?   Its silence seems
To frown on me, and to reproach in tones
Of holy innocence my deep-laid crime.
I'd hold a parley with it if I dared,
But I should fear to hear me speak.   And yet
I've gone too far to wrest the murderous hand.
My wife will be in heaven ere long.   The scheme
Is too well laid to fear its non-success.
And yet I love her ! she is worthy me.
She is as virtuous as she is beautiful ;
She is, indeed, a paragon of wives.
I'd sound her praises with my dying breath.
Yet I must kill her, for her living means

A life imprisonment for me, or death.
I cannot sacrifice my life for hers,
For she would never sacrifice herself
For me.   Is it not better she were dead,
Than be deprived of me and liberty,
And live a ling'ring, tortured life within
The Tower?   In killing her am I not kind?
She'll die, at least, in painless innocence.
For me I see, in spite of all its joys,
A weary life.   Where is that happy man
Who drags a guilty conscience?

Enter MURDERER.

Thou com'st!   Why dost thou drag thy steps?

MURDERER.

A heavy weight doth make them slow.

LEICESTER.

    Come, cheer up, man.
Do all thy crimes affect thee thus?

MURDERER.

     Nay, otherwise.

LEICESTER.

What dost thou mean?

MURDERER.

     They give me speed.

LEICESTER.

Then, why has this not quickened thee?

MURDERER.

Because it is not done.

LEICESTER.

Not done!

Did courage fail thee at the last?

MURDERER.

Thou told'st me she would be alone.

LEICESTER.

She is!

MURDERER.

Thou liest!

LEICESTER.

I lie?

Whom didst thou see with her?

MURDERER.

A man.

LEICESTER.

Nay!

MURDERER.

> A man, I say.

LEICESTER.

> Great God!
And is she false to me? Yea, she shall die,
Though I must do the deed myself. Come, friend,
We'll kill them both in their adultery. (*Aside*)
I'm glad on this, for I've a deeper cause
Why she should die.

MURDERER.

> I will not come with thee.

LEICESTER.

> Why, coward?
Hast thou not pluck enough to meet a man?

MURDERER.

I've pluck enough to meet a man, but not
An army of them.

LEICESTER.

> An army?
Pray, speak in simpler words, my friend. (*Aside*)
I fear some plot against my life.

MURDERER.

> In short, 'tis this:
As I approached, a dozen horsemen reached

The house, demanding in our sovereign's name
Admittance. The door was oped, and in they
    walked.
They stayed inside a grievous time.   At last
They ushered forth, but with thy screaming wife,
With whom they quickly rode away.

LEICESTER.
Is that thy tale ?

MURDERER.

It briefly pictures what I saw.

LEICESTER.
It is a mystery
I cannot solve.   Didst hear no words by which
Thou couldst detect their errand ?

MURDERER.

No word was uttered.

LEICESTER.
I'd give my life
If I could know these men.

MURDERER.

Methinks thou never wilt.
[*Exeunt both.*

SCENE III.—*A street in London.*

Enter FÉNELON *and* LINCOLN.

FÉNELON.

We have his wife, I say,
And surer evidence thou couldst not get.

LINCOLN.

When wilt thou tell the queen
He hath a living wife?

FÉNELON.

Depend on it,
I'll choose a time quite suitable.

LINCOLN.

I would the secret were not kept from her
For many hours.

FÉNELON.

It shall not, rest assured.

LINCOLN.

O Leicester, thy great fall is near!

FÉNELON.

'Twill crush him past all recognising him.

LINCOLN.

Nay, can he fall from such a height and live ?

FÉNELON.

He hath much life in him.

[*Exeunt both.*

SCENE IV.—*An apartment in the Palace. Enter*
LADY SHEFFIELD *and* FRANCES HOWARD.

LADY SHEFFIELD.

A storm indeed ! ha ! ha !
There'll be the greatest storm these walls have
    heard.
Oh, how her majesty will rave at him !

FRANCES HOWARD.

Poor Leicester !

LADY SHEFFIELD.

And dost thou pity him ?

FRANCES HOWARD.

Did I not smile in uttering it ?   Indeed,
I've scarcely known a happier day.

LADY SHEFFIELD.

And yet thou lov'st him !

FRANCES HOWARD.

And thou art jealous of his wife. It is
Her punishment that pleases thee.

LADY SHEFFIELD.

Yet I have never done what thou hast done.

FRANCES HOWARD.

I've never stooped as thou hast stooped. I've
held
My head above my knees, indeed.

LADY SHEFFIELD.

'Twas but to let him see thy glassy eyes.

FRANCES HOWARD.

If thou hadst shown him thine he would have
scorned
So vile an imitation.

LADY SHEFFIELD.

I've heard him laugh at thee.

FRANCES HOWARD.

Because I pleased my lord. When thou cam'st
near,
His happy look did change to grief.

LADY SHEFFIELD.

Thou art a saucy wench.

FRANCES HOWARD.

And thou a fiery one.

[*Exeunt the two ladies.*

Enter ELIZABETH *and* SIR CHARLES HATTON.

ELIZABETH.

'Tis jealousy disturbing thee again.
Some men are overheated with strong wine,
But envy hath inflamed thy heart and mind,
And made thee use these incoherent words.

HATTON.

Nay, madam, thou dost wrongly rate me thus.
By heaven! thou dost. My head's as cool as
     thine.
I will confess my heart is warm ; nay, that
It is inflamed. I'll swear by Holy Writ
It is not jealousy that heats it thus.
'Tis love for thee ; yea, truest love, sweet lady—
No counterfeit, by all that's true. 'Tis love
That longs for thy great joy and happiness.

ELIZABETH.

Then, rest assured I am a happy queen.

HATTON.

Thou art not ; nay, thou canst not be.

ELIZABETH.

What hinders it ?

HATTON.

Thou'lt say I'm envious if I tell it thee.

ELIZABETH.

I bid thee speak.

HATTON.

Thou hast deep love for him who scorns thee.

ELIZABETH.

And who is he ?

HATTON.

Nay, wilt thou ask ?

ELIZABETH.

Have I not asked ?

HATTON.

Thou lovest Leicester, who's not worthy thee.

ELIZABETH.

Who says I love him ?   Have I said myself ?

HATTON.

Thou hast not, lady, but thy acts express
Deep love for him.

ELIZABETH.

It is thy wilful misinterpretation.

HATTON.

Not mine alone, sweet lady; others have
Observed, and marked them too, with meaning
nods.
And wilt thou say they misinterpret thee?

ELIZABETH.

Who are these men
Who watch me thus?   By God! I'll make them
spies!

HATTON.

They are not spies.   They cannot shut their
eyes
To what is done before them.   They must see,
Or else be wilful blind.

ELIZABETH.

I say,
They make it their one aim in life to mark
My acts, to spy me out.   I know them well.

12

Dost think I have not marked their frowns and
    seen
Their scornful smiles ?   God's death !   I'll see
    their tears
Ere long.   Another pastime they shall have,
But not where sunshine comes.

HATTON.

It is their duty, madam.
It proves their faithfulness.

ELIZABETH.
What !
Dost take me for a dolt ?   This is no sign
Of love, my friend.   Thou canst not flatter me
With such sweet words. I know ambition's ways.
It is a quality that plots and schemes.
Thou canst not teach me what it loves.

HATTON.

Ambition that doth plot to serve its queen,
And to preserve herself and throne from those
Who seek to ruin them, doth seem to me
A worthy spectacle.   The greatest nation
Is that where such ambition is.

ELIZABETH.

Thou speakest truthfully,
But that ambition which doth strive—nor minds

The means—to raise itself, and doth regard
With jealous eye the height which others have
Attained, will, if not checked at first, do harm.
'Tis that which hath destroyed the greatest
  nations,
Though they were built upon unselfishness
At first. Yea, I must cure such jealousy.
I'll have no weeds where flowers may grow.

HATTON.

Pray, pardon me.
Thou dost not doubt my love?

ELIZABETH.

Well, crush this jealousy, or else I'll look
On thee as one who loves thyself with strength
That doth not suit humility.

[*Exit* HATTON.

Go, feeble man,
And tempt me not. Oh, God! why am I plagued
With such weak-minded men? Is it a curse
Pronounced against unwedded life? 'Tis they
Who are to blame for my unmarried state.
'Tis they who've been the shadows of my life,
The threat'ning clouds which have obscured the
  sun,
And made my path a dull, uncertain one.
Where'er I go their faces haunt me; yea,

With ugly menace, too. They're cowards all.
They know a king would fill their hearts with fear,
And so they'd have me be their humble queen.
I'll show them yet I can put on the man.
I'll make them quake. God's blood! I'll let them
    know
No feeble woman governs them.

                    [*Exit* ELIZABETH.

       Enter SUSSEX *and* BURLEIGH.

           SUSSEX.

                I pity him.
Her anger will demand his instant death.
The blow will be so sudden and so strange
That it will crush all womanly tenderness,
And make her heart a stone. She'll look on him
As on a monster worthy scorn and hate.
And this will last for days and weeks, until
She doth regain her womanliness and show
Repentance and remorse. She then will grieve
O'er Leicester's death, and be the constant prey
Of melancholy. Burleigh, we must save
Our blessed queen. She must not do the deeds
Of sudden madness, and suffer the remorse
Of sanity regained. Nor do I long
For Leicester's death; I bear him no ill will
Of deadly quality. His game is o'er;

His power is crushed.   Henceforth he'll be too
    weak
To do our queen and country harm.   With that
I'll be content.

BURLEIGH.

I'd rather see him dead.   Nor do I think
The queen will suffer all the agony
Thou hast depicted.   But I long to know,
Ere further words are said, what is the scheme
Thou dost propose to save his head.

SUSSEX.

To use our influence and counsel her
To stay the axe.   To send him far away,
On pain of putting him to death if he
Return.   'Twill be a task, I must confess,
Of subtlest delicacy and hazard, yet
I'm sanguine of success.

BURLEIGH.

Thou'rt ever sanguine, Sussex; yea, too sanguine.
I know of none so happy in his hopes
Of sure success, yet it doth not have source
In ever fruitfulness.   I say, we should
Incur the queen's displeasure if at such
A time we tendered such advice.   Yea, far
From soothing her, as is thy wish, we would
But add more fuel to the fire, in which

She'd also scorch us up. 'Twere wise of us
To keep at distance safe, and let her fury
Destroy the cause of it.

SUSSEX.

This is no manly talk, my worthy lord.
I know thou art not well, or else such words
Would never leave thy lips. There is a duty
We owe to her which should not dread her ire.
I know thou wilt recall thy words, and thus
I rest contented thou wilt come.

BURLEIGH.

I've said what I intend. This man hath done
Already grievous injury to me,
And I were mad, indeed, to lift him up
That he might strike at me again. Nay, nay.
Count not on me to be his advocate.

SUSSEX.

How can he injure thee again ? He's down,
To rise no more. He'll have no power to strike.
Nay, Burleigh, this is no excuse. I say,
Thy health hath much enfeebled thee. To-
    morrow
Thou'lt be another man.

BURLEIGH.

I've said what I've resolved.

[*Exeunt both.*

Enter ELIZABETH *with* LEICESTER.

ELIZABETH.

Thou hast thy enemies, but never fear,
For I will be thy shield.   To see thee fall
Would give them thrilling joy.   For them such
    joy
Shall never be.

LEICESTER.

       I thank thee, madam ;
Such gracious words do fill my heart with hope.
Thou art the staff on which I must depend
For life ; yea, life, for if they had their wish
I should not now be in thy queenly presence.

ELIZABETH.

       I know it, Leicester.
I know they wish thee dead ; but whilst I live
Thou never need'st fear death from thy base foes.

LEICESTER.

       Again I thank thee.
Thou ever hast been wondrous kind to him
Who is not worthy e'en to kneel to thee.

Thou art the only friend I have, sweet lady,
Yet thou art more than many.   How I long
To pay in love and true allegiance
The debt I owe to thee !   It is a debt
I cannot find fit language to express.
I ask thee, do I merit all their hate ?
Would they regard me with such jealousy
If thou didst frown on me ?   Nay, nay !   I'd be
A thing contemptible.   I feel the brunt
Of their displeasure with thy gracious looks
And words.   Thy graciousness to me hath bred
This hatred in their jealous hearts.   If they
Regard me with this evil eye, they must
Assume their fond regards for thee.

ELIZABETH.

I know it.

'Tis all hypocrisy.   They hate me too.
Yea, I have searched their faithless hearts ere
        now,
And seen the falseness there.   Thank God, I
        know
A certain cure for this, which I'll apply
Ere many days are o'er.

LEICESTER.

'Twould be most wise.
Delay might make the evil past all cure.

I know they've tried to poison thee with lies
That I have likewise been a faithless subject,
And I have spent most grievous, painful hours
In thinking that to thee their words might bear
The stamp of truth.   Yet with great joy I've
    seen
That thou hast read their hearts aright, and hast
Displayed the wisdom which a loving God
Hath blessed thee with.   I've heard of foolish
    queens
Who have been led astray by hypocrites
And flatterers, who did disguise their hate
With the attractive garb of love.   But thou
Hast vision which can pierce all falsehood's guise,
However skilfully it be portrayed.
That is the source of thy prosperity,
Which none before thee ever knew.

ELIZABETH.

Ah, Leicester, thou didst ever think too well
Of me.   I am not worthy of such praise.
I have some gifts, I know, but not so great
As thou dost say I frequently display.
I've been deceived e'er now.

LEICESTER.

But not for long, sweet lady ; thou hast found
Thy error out before great harm was done.

Canst thou or anyone look round and mark
The evidence of any foolish act ?
Can they point finger at the least defect,
And say, ' If she had had a keener eye,
Or deeper mind, this never would have been ' ?
Nay, lady. That's the sum and evidence
Of all true wisdom and of intellect,
Which thou hast got in perfect measure.

ELIZABETH.

I must not let thee prattle on so fast,
Or else thou'lt make me out divine.

LEICESTER.

      Thou art.
I ofttimes think in my most serious moments
That God hath sent thee down from heaven to us
To rule the country which He loves, that He
Might thus reward its faith. Thou art so perfect,
Thou scarcely seemest human.

ELIZABETH.

Alas ! I would I were less human.

LEICESTER.

    I'm glad thou'rt not, indeed.
It is a blessing for this mighty land.
Thou'lt pardon me—for it will show I have

A human weakness—hast thou ever had
A doubt of my allegiance to thee?

ELIZABETH.

Nay, never, Leicester;
No thought of that e'er grieved my heart. Why dost
Thou question it?

LEICESTER.

I know not, lady,
Except it was to hear from thy sweet lips
That thou dost still have trust in me.

ELIZABETH.

Then, be assured I have and will until——

LEICESTER.

Until——

ELIZABETH.

Thou dost deceive me.

LEICESTER.

Deceive thee!
Dost think I ever could?

ELIZABETH.

'Tis possible.

LEICESTER.

Nay, lady, never.
I'd leave my country first.

ELIZABETH.
Pray God thou never wilt.

LEICESTER.

Amen !

[*Exeunt both.*

SCENE V.—*Outside the Palace.*

Enter TWO GENTLEMEN, *meeting.*

1ST GENT.

Good-morrow, friend.

2ND GENT.
Good-morrow, my good sir.

1ST GENT.

It is a pleasant morn.

2ND GENT.
To some ; to one it is a woful morn.
Thou knowest what has happened, friend ?

1st Gent.

Nay, who can tell?
Storms come so suddenly upon us now,
That never have we cause to boast of times
Of sunshine, which oft disappears e'en whilst
We're praising it.   So how can anyone
Boast knowledge of events?

2nd Gent.

But one event has happened, friend, which is
The topic of all serious talk.   Thou sure
Hast heard of it?

1st Gent.

But she hath thrown a lover off ere now.
Why take this latest freak so seriously?

2nd Gent.

I see thou hast not learnt the newest thing.
I must enlighten thee.   Wouldst ever dream
That Leicester had a wife?

1st Gent.

Nay, friend.
Restraint so great would ne'er exhaust his lust.
A dozen wives would make him virtuous.

2ND GENT.

But he is really wed.

1ST GENT.

By parson ?

2ND GENT.

By church and ring.

1ST GENT.

It cannot be.

2ND GENT.

And, pray, why not ?

1ST GENT.

The church would fall on him.

2ND GENT.

It hath not, friend.

1ST GENT.

Then he's not married.

2ND GENT.

I tell thee that he is,
And I have seen his wife—I mean the queen
Hath looked on her.

1ST GENT.

How hath she punished her ?

2ND GENT.

She's imprisoned in the Tower.

1ST GENT.

Her true deserts.

2ND GENT.

Thou hast a cruel heart.

1ST GENT.

I have no sympathy for those true fools
Who worship such a man.   A child could read
His lying, vain, and vicious heart.

2ND GENT.

The world will never see him more.

1ST GENT.

Methinks it will.

2ND GENT.

The queen will not o'erlook the deed.

1ST GENT.

Who knows her mind?
What skill can read her changing heart?

[*Exeunt both.*

SCENE VI.—*An apartment in the Palace.*

Enter the QUEEN *and* LEICESTER.

ELIZABETH.

        Plead not with me, I say.
What canst thou urge t'excuse a trait'rous heart?
What words can blot away the hideous stain
On thy false heart? Thou art as black as hell
Is hot, thou perjured hypocrite!

LEICESTER.

        When I am dead
Thou wilt repent these words.

ELIZABETH.

        Repent them, traitor!
Dost thou repent thy lies?

LEICESTER.

        I do repent them, lady;
But thou wilt pay no heed to what I say.

ELIZABETH.

        No heed! God's death!
Dost think I'd heed thy falsehoods now? Alas!
I do repent I ever heeded them.

Oh, how this man hath made me his scorned
    tool !
How he hath mocked, and laughed, and jeered
    at me
From that proud height to which I mounted
    him !
The love he did pretend for me was hate ;
And I put faith in all his boasted lies !
Ha, fiend ! I have thee now ! Thou'rt safe !
    by God,
Thou shalt not keep thy wicked head !

LEICESTER.

Why dost thou tie my tongue ?

ELIZABETH.

Oh, would that I had silenced it ere now !
I would have saved myself this cruel grief !
I would have heard less lies ! This palace would
Have been a purer place ! I say, thou hast
Polluted it with thy foul breath. To think
That I have breathed the air which thou hast
    breathed !
O God, why didst Thou send this scourge to me,
This scorpion, to sting my life ? I'll rid

The world of it, that it may never know
The pain of its foul sting again.

Enter BURLEIGH *and* HATTON, *who listen at a
distance.*

LEICESTER.

      Thou art unjust to me.
I thought thou wert a fairer queen.

ELIZABETH.

        Unjust to thee!
Hast thou been just or fair to me? Dost thou
Deserve for all thy crimes, for all the deeds
Of sin that thou hast done, a lenient
And pitying regard? Yea, yea, thou dost!
Thy cowardliness doth seek for pity from
The heart it bruised. Thou art a perfect coward,
As thou art perfect in hypocrisy.
The coward hath a loud and pleading tongue,
But bravery a silent, pleading heart.
Oh, why was I so blind as not to see
Thou didst disguise thyself in bravery's garb!

LEICESTER.

      How can I soften thee?

Others come in and stand at a distance.

ELIZABETH.

Thou never wilt.
Nay, kneeling will more harden me.   I'm proof
Against all supplicating postures, which
Doth evidence thou art an arrant cur.

LEICESTER.

I know thou'lt not forgive me, lady; all
I ask is that I may retain my head.
I would die whole.   I cannot live for long
If banished from thy face.   In solitude,
And far from thee, I'd be as one that's dead,
Which is thy wish.

ELIZABETH.

Nay, nay;
I'll be convinced thou'rt dead.   I'll see thy corpse
And ease my mind.   Thou'rt not the man to hide
In solitude.   Thou wouldst conspire against
My life, wouldst plot and scheme to seek revenge.
I know thy cowardly heart.   If when I smiled
On thee thou didst thy best to injure me,
How wouldst thou harm me when I frown on
thee !
I've trusted thee too long.   I do repent
I e'er put faith in thee.

LEICESTER.

Oh, canst thou not be merciful?

ELIZABETH.

Go, wretch,

And let me gaze on thee no more.

LEICESTER.

Nay, but one word.

ELIZABETH.

Go!

Or 'twill be worse for thee.

LEICESTER.

Alas!

Thou knowest not thou art thyself to blame.
If thou——

(ELIZABETH, *in a tempest of wrath, leaves him. The curtain falls on* LEICESTER'S *discomfiture and prostration.*)

Elliot Stock, Paternoster Row London.